"I—I am a friend of your wife."

Violet could not keep the challenging note out of her voice.

"Are you, my lady? Yes, I believe I have heard her mention your name," he said.

She sank onto the bench, her knees giving way. He did not know her cousin. Her secret was safe for the nonce. But the sooner she put a distance between herself and this intriguing—and married!—man, the happier she would be.

"I myself am bethrothed," she offered.

"Who knows 'What next morn's sun may bring,'" he murmured, as though to himself.

She looked up, startled. "I beg your pardon?"

"Naught," he said. "Mere maundering. Shall we go inside?"

Violet was quick to agree. After all, she reasoned, there was safety in numbers.

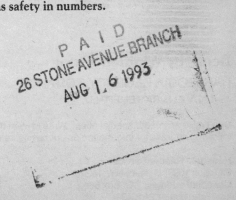

Books by Winifred Witton

HARLEQUIN REGENCY ROMANCE
46–LADY ELMIRA'S EMERALD

THE DENVILLE DIAMOND

WINIFRED WITTON

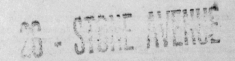

Harlequin Books

TORONTO • NEW YORK • LONDON
AMSTERDAM • PARIS • SYDNEY • HAMBURG
STOCKHOLM • ATHENS • TOKYO • MILAN

For Marmie

Published July 1991

ISBN 0-373-31154-0

THE DENVILLE DIAMOND

CHAPTER ONE

MISS VIOLET LANGFORD squinted, near-sighted, at the names of the shops she passed. She was nervous as she proceeded towards Hookam's Lending Library and she clutched her reticule tightly, casting suspicious glances at the gentlemen who passed. Being a poor relation, she had no abigail to accompany her.

Ordinarily, her cousin made her woman available for such trips into Town. Violet felt a little comforting rush of warmth. Dear Cousin Clarissa had rescued her from the drab life of a vicar's third daughter by employing her as companion, but she had to admit that sometimes Lady Clarissa Langford was a trifle thoughtless. However, she was deeply beholden to that flighty young lady and had no right to complain. Also, it was her own fault entirely that she had mislaid the thick spectacles, which were her constant companion, and had to peer at the names of the streets. She quickened her steps; only think if she were to miss the turning to the library and become quite lost!

She caught a breath of relief. Surely that was Lord Ralston's son Montrose just ahead! Even from the great distance of ten paces or more she was certain she recognized the set of his padded shoulders, his nipped-in waist and the ridiculous beehive hat he had worn on his last visit to Langford House. Montrose, the fiancé of Lady Clarissa, would provide safe escort. She hurried up to him and caught his sleeve.

"Thank heaven. I have been feeling so alone!"

The man turned and gaped at her, bleary-eyed. Violet shrieked in terror. Not Montrose! A complete stranger, and one in his cups at that!

With a loose-mouthed leer, he caught her wrist and pulled her into his arms.

"You ain't alone anymore!"

She shrieked again, struggling in vain in the man's odious grip. His wet mouth streaked across her forehead and landed on her ear as she twisted her face away. Her arms were pinned to her chest, and though she kicked valiantly at his shins, she wore only her soft slippers. Oh, why had she not donned heavier half-boots!

Then, just as she had quite given her virtue up for lost, a tall gentleman with a shock of red hair seized her assailant by the back of his collar and the seat of his breeches and tossed him into the gutter.

The drunken man struggled to his feet, his fists raised, but the lanky figure towered a full head over him. Violet covered her ears with both hands as her attacker muttered what was no doubt an expletive unfit for a lady to hear. He left the scene with what dignity he could muster.

She turned to her rescuer gratefully, straightening the dowdy bonnet on her light brown hair. "Sir, I cannot thank you enough!" She realized belatedly that she should have fainted in a ladylike manner instead of offering him her hand, but he seemed to perceive nothing amiss.

"Delighted to have been of service," he said, bending over her trembling fingers in a graceful bow. "I trust our erstwhile companion was not an acquaintance?"

"Oh, no! No indeed! I was walking by myself."

He shook his head disapprovingly. "That will never do. 'Beauty provoketh thieves sooner than gold.'"

Violet nodded. "Shakespeare. *As You Like It,* Act One," she replied knowledgeably. "But I am afraid I am no beauty."

He narrowed his eyes and peered at her, almost as though he were as near-sighted as she. "'There is a garden in her face, Where roses and white lilies blow.' You look quite well enough to me."

She giggled, surprised to feel as giddy as Cousin Clarissa. Not at all a staid four-and-twenty!

"'There cherries grow that none may buy, Till Cherry-ripe themselves do cry.'" She finished the verse, pleased at his obvious delight in her quick recognition of the quote.

He offered her his arm with a warm smile. "I had best escort you to your destination. Though I doubt our unpleasant friend will return. 'The thief doth fear each bush an officer.'"

"Now where is that from?" she asked, genuinely interested. "Though I must say it is not quite applicable. He stole nothing from me."

He grinned. "Lurched, eh? Shakespeare again. *Henry VI,* Part 3, to be exact."

"I bow to your superior scholarship, sir. May I know your name that I may thank you properly?"

"Oh, Lord, I have forgot my manners." He flushed brick-red to the roots of his flaming hair, exhibiting a vulnerability she found completely endearing. He made her another elegant bow. "Bentley Frome, ma'am, your most obedient servant."

Her most *charming* servant, she thought as she curtsied in return. "And I am Violet Langford." His name was familiar. She wrinkled her brow for a moment. "Frome... are you related to the Earl of Denville, then?"

"My brother, for my sins. Do you know him?"

"I—I have heard of him." She realized she had hesitated a second too long, for she sensed his sudden withdrawal. "My cousin Clarissa is well acquainted with his wife," she added hastily.

"I trust you will not believe all you hear," he said a bit stiffly. "Though I admit Hildebrand was a trifle high-spirited before his marriage."

High-spirited! Violet's lips tightened. High-spirited indeed, if only half the tales she had heard were true!

"Hildebrand is a great gun," Bentley Frome went on earnestly. "Now that he is wed and settled down, he is a different man, I assure you."

They had reached the library door, and they spoke for only a few more minutes. When she bade him farewell, "with a smile on her lips and a tear in her eye," she felt that grateful tear come perilously close.

Surely, "there never was knight like the young Lochinvar" who had so gallantly come to her rescue. She was hopelessly mixing her quotes, but then she felt quite hopelessly mixed herself.

Warm colour flowed to her cheeks as she bent over one of the book tables inside, squinting in an effort to decipher the titles. What inestimable luck that she had mislaid her spectacles and was not wearing them during her encounter with her "verray, parfit gentil knyght!" He'd never have been so delightful a companion, so attentive, to a lady in spectacles.

Not for the world would she have had him know her for the compleat bluestocking she was!

THE HONOURABLE Bentley Frome, Cambridge don and fellow, with a grant for the study of poetry and drama, replaced on his aquiline nose the spectacles he had shoved into his pocket before dashing into the fray. His soft brown eyes were vague, for behind his thick lenses a bevy of knights in shining armour slew flame-breathing dragons and rescued damsels in distress. He himself wore no armour, of course. It was no longer in style, and he was not a man to take the tenets of the ton lightly. He was instead impeccably dressed for a morning visit to his sister-in-law, the Countess of Denville, who had sent him an urgent summons.

But he *had* rescued a bona fide damsel in distress! What would Lochinvar have done? Or the Corsair? Or, for that matter, any of his poetic heroes? They would have tucked their spectacles into their pockets and leaped to the rescue of the fair maiden just as he had done. With difficulty he prevented himself from prancing down Bond Street, as though astride a destrier with his pennant flying above his head.

His exalted mood had not diminished by the time he arrived at Frome House, the London home of his brother, the Earl of Denville, and he gave the gleaming brass knocker a hearty bang. The great oaken door flew open, and with a flurry of muslin ruffles and dusky curls, his young sister-in-law threw herself into his arms and burst into theatrical sobs.

"Devil take it, Letty," he complained. "You make us 'the cynosure of neighbouring eyes!' Do strive for a little restraint." Conscious of the butler, two footmen and a housemaid all gaping at them, Bentley disentangled himself and led the weeping Letitia back into the house. Once inside the nearest drawing-room, he shut the door firmly on the goggling domestics, adjusted his gold-rimmed spectacles and removed a shallow-crowned beaver from his carefully disordered red curls. He set it on a rosewood boulle table and faced the distraught lady.

"Now what?" he demanded with a familiar sense of resignation. "Hard-pressed by your mantua maker? Blown all your blunt again?"

"Worse!" she wailed. "The most terrible coil I've ever fallen into and I'll die if Hildebrand finds out!"

Bentley removed the thick-lensed spectacles and polished them on his coat sleeve before replacing them. "I fail to see where anything a chit like you could do would shock him," he remarked mildly.

A confirmed rake, Hildebrand, fifth Earl of Denville, had been in and out of trouble all his expensive life until, at the age of five-and-thirty, he had married Lady Letitia, a maiden barely seventeen. Since then he had been a pattern-card of propriety, astounding the ton as well as Bentley, who had begun to fear that the necessity of producing an heir would descend on him.

Letitia sniffed loudly into a scrap of lace, and he handed her his more practical linen handkerchief. She promptly buried her face in it and sank onto a sofa.

"Come, Letty," he rallied her. "You're not usually such a watering pot." Seating himself beside her, he drew her into his arms, patting at her comfortingly here and there. "Dry your eyes. 'Nothing is here for tears, nothing to wail or knock the—'" He coughed suddenly, remembering the next word. "I make no doubt you are but enacting me a Cheltenham tragedy and we may soon settle the affair. At the moment, however," he went on conversationally, "you are ruining my neckcloth. And only think, suppose Hildebrand were to come in at this moment and find me cuddling you. He would be beset by 'surmises, jealousies, conjectures.'"

He was rewarded by a weak giggle from Letitia, who was accustomed to the literary turn of his conversation. "I knew I could count on you, Bentley, and there is no one else I can trust in this matter."

He stifled a sigh. That was his problem. Ever chivalrous, ever trustworthy, he was considered by all his acquaintance a solid rock to be clung to and confided in. Idly, he wondered what good confiding in a rock would do one. He must try it sometime.

Letitia stirred, scrubbing her cheek against his shoulder, and he pushed her a little away.

"My new coat may never recover. Tell me all and let us end your misery while my garments are still salvageable."

She raised her tear-streaked face. "You must help me! Promise!"

"Anything within my power. That is—" he eyed her uneasily "—anything within reason."

"Oh, it is of all things the *most* unreasonable. My whole dependence is upon you."

Bentley ran a hand through his red hair, disarranging his *au coup de vent*. "Letty, how can I help until I know the problem?"

"Piquet!" she pronounced tragically.

He nodded. "I take it you have been gaming. How much do you need this time?"

"Money! If it were only that! Oh, Bentley, I shall have to retire to the country and be immured in the highest tower room of Frome for the rest of my life! I will die at once!"

"In that case, at least your 'durance vile' will be of short duration."

At this callous comment, she stiffened. "I beg you will not be flippant! I am quite serious and I truly need your aid."

"All right. No doubt, like Athenaeus, I will have seen 'a more formidable storm in a boiling saucepan.' Give me the whole tale without roundaboutation."

Letitia caught his hand and pressed it urgently. "It came about in the most insidious way. You see, while Hildebrand was out of Town for a few weeks, I began going to a very respectable house—in Grosvenor Street! Quite discreet parties, you must know, only there was gaming."

Bentley gave her a disapproving look. "You should never have gone to such a place, Letty. 'For there's nae luck about the house, There's nae luck at a', There's little pleasure—'"

She shushed him impatiently. "Yes, yes. That's as may be. But I did go, and I ran up a perfectly horrendous debt and pledged the Denville diamond."

"You—what?" He yanked his hand away.

"Oh, not really, Bent," she reassured him. "You see, the brooch I had on was a paste copy. Hildebrand will never allow me to wear the genuine diamond except to formal balls."

"I cannot blame him!"

Letitia nodded. "Besides, I truly never meant to pledge it."

Bentley looked at her helplessly. "Then, for mercy's sake, why did you?"

"It was all Lord Ralston's fault! He held my vowels in the amount of almost a thousand pounds and he demanded the diamond as security."

"You should have refused." Bentley frowned. "He'd know Hildebrand would settle with him."

"Oh, but he promised I could redeem it, when I received my quarterly allowance the very next week, so Hildebrand would never find out! Hildebrand will slay me if he learns I have been gaming after the last time. But knowing the stone was paste somehow removed my caution...."

Bentley rolled his eyes heavenward. "Of course."

"I have worn the copy so often and have had it accepted as the original by one and all that even I sometimes forget it is not the real brooch. Lord Ralston doesn't know it is the *faux,* and now he refuses to return it! He says he won it fair and square, and threatens to go to my husband and tell all if I continue to beg for it back. I pleaded with him not to tell Hildebrand, and I daresay Ralston will not, but he told me he plans to have the stone appraised. I will be exposed as a pledger of false coin and he will denounce me before the ton as a—a thimblerigger! Bentley, you must get that brooch back for me!"

"How the devil am I to do that?" Bentley ran both hands through his already ravaged hair. "Good God, Letty, whatever made you think you could play piquet?"

"I always win from Hildebrand!"

"Well, that's nothing to speak of. He can't play worth a damn. Hasn't the mind for card games."

"Bentley, I think Lord Ralston was cheating."

"Don't be a goosecap. Why would a respected gentleman, old enough to be your father, cheat a silly chit like you?"

Letitia spread her hands in a hopeless gesture. "He must have. I cannot understand how else it happened. I was winning—so much!—and then... Oh, I'll

never play piquet or silver loo or even backgammon
ever again!''

"It's too late now, the deed is done. I can do no
more than speak to Lord Ralston on your behalf."
Bentley rose and paced about the room. "I will offer
him more than your debt and point out the well-
known fact that the Denville diamond is an heirloom
and not yours to pledge. If he has any honour at all,
he will return the brooch."

"I tried that," said Letitia. "He laughed at me."

Bentley hesitated, considering her thoughtfully.
"You think he fuzzed the cards, eh? And he's gone
back on his word. Verily, 'a hungry, lean-fac'd villain.'"

"Yes, and you must see there is nothing for it but
for you to get my paste diamond away from him before he has it appraised."

"But how in blazes do you expect me to do that?"

Letitia caught his hand and pulled him down onto
the sofa again. "I have been giving the problem a great
deal of thought. We have a week, for Lord Ralston is
hosting a race-meet party at his country estate, Branleigh. I know because Hildebrand and I received an
invitation weeks ago."

"Ralston invited Hildebrand?" Bentley shook his
head. "I understand he was requested to leave on his
last visit nearly five years ago."

"I know. The dowager called him a dashed libertine." Letitia giggled. "But Hildebrand said it was
only that they had a remarkably pretty housemaid,

and when he stole a kiss under the stairs, the old harridan caught him.''

Shocked, Bentley blinked at her through his spectacles. ''He told you that?''

''Of course. It was long before he met me. And he has quite settled down now. Lady Hippolyta must feel that since he has become leg-shackled he is socially acceptable once more.''

Bentley pursed his lips. ''Really, Letty, you should not use cant.''

''Only to you, my dear. You would never betray me.''

''Just so.'' Bentley tried to look disapproving and gave up. ''However, I cannot imagine why Lady Hippolyta allowed him to be invited back.''

''It was at the request of Sir Henry Field, who is another nephew of hers. He insisted Hildebrand be there to alleviate the utterly abysmal dullness of the rest of the company. But now Sir Henry has come down with a convenient chill and has an excuse not to go. But he has asked Hildebrand to attend anyway, to put a monkey on some nag or other for him at the races. If only they had invited you instead of Hildebrand...'' She cast him a sideways glance through her long lashes, and Bentley's brows snapped together.

''Letty, why are you looking at me like that? I am reminded of Macbeth. 'By the pricking of my thumbs, Something wicked this way comes—' ''

''No, no! Really, it is just that I have thought of a way for you to get into Branleigh and steal back my brooch.''

"What?"

"They do not know Hildebrand all that well. It has been five years, after all. You shall go in his place, masquerading as him!"

"Letitia, you have taken leave of your senses."

"That I have not!" She bounced on the sofa. "Only think, once you are there it will be a simple matter to find where Lord Ralston has placed my brooch and to pocket it. Then you may leave immediately."

"Compounding your crime? No, I will not! Besides the fact that I do not look like Hildebrand, he will be there himself."

"No, he won't, for I shall tell him I cannot go because I am increasing at last, and then he will not leave my side."

"You cannot get away with such a bouncer!"

Letitia blushed. "It is no such thing. I *am* in the family way, but he does not know as yet." She dimpled, a picture of mischief. "I have been saving the news for just such an emergency as this."

"Letty, you are incorrigible!"

She beamed at him. "I know. Is it not fortunate?"

"This does not solve all. There is still an insurmountable difficulty. No one would take me for Hildebrand. For one thing, he is dark, and I fear my hair is decidedly on the auburn side."

But Letitia had already considered the problem. Reaching up, she snatched off his spectacles before he could stop her.

"You look very much like Hildebrand without your eyeglasses. Only look in the mirror!"

Bentley blinked vaguely about the suddenly blurred room. "Where?"

"There." She spun him around. "Over the mantel. See? Without your spectacles, and with your hair dyed black, you can pass for him easily."

Bentley found the mirror and peered at himself. He did look startlingly like Hildebrand except for his colouring. He raised another objection. "Hildebrand has a moustache." The moustache was a relic of his brother's two years on the Continent with Wellington, before he succeeded to the title. Considering it rather dashing, the new Earl of Denville had flown in the face of Brummel's fashion and refused to shave it off, much to Bentley's disgust. "There is no way I could grow such a ghastly hirsute appendage in only one week."

"You must wear a false one, of course!"

"And where am I to come by a false moustache?"

"Why," said Letitia, her blue eyes wide and innocent, "I have one." She skipped to the Queen Anne desk in the corner and produced a repellent handful of black hair.

Bentley recoiled. "Good God!"

Letitia turned to the mirror, arranging the moustache on her own charming face. "This belonged to a friend of Hildebrand's. He considered it lucky and always wore it while playing at cards, until one night at a party here, when he lost heavily and threw it away. Naturally I retrieved it, for I have always wanted to see how I would look as a man."

"Naturally." Bentley fixed her with an accusing, albeit myopic, eye. "Letitia, you had this planned all along."

She blinked at him over the lush facial adornment. "Of course. How else am I to come about?"

"I should look an absolute fool in that thing!"

"No, indeed!" She removed the moustache and tried to put it on him. "Only see, it fits quite neatly. It is backed by some sticky substance, so you merely press it to your upper lip."

He pushed it away. "Never!" He thought of another objection, a powerful one. "I'd never be able to copy Hildebrand's style of neckcloths. He sports an *orientale* or a *trône d'amour* and I've always worn a simple mathematical."

Ready tears sprang once more to Letitia's aid. She allowed them to trickle down as though unheeded. Bentley shuffled his feet unhappily and took refuge once more in Macbeth.

"'Why do I yield to that suggestion Whose horrid image doth unfix my hair—'"

Letitia scrubbed at her wet cheeks with the back of her hand. "You messed it up yourself. Here, put on your spectacles and you may repair the damage."

"'And make my seated heart knock at my ribs?'" he completed the quotation. "Letty, this whole idea is impossible. I cannot go to a man's home and steal from him!"

"It would be no such thing! You would merely be taking back an object stolen from me by cheating!"

"There is no proof that the man cheated."

The tears flowed again, and she attached herself to his crumpled lapels. "Bentley, only think what will happen to me if you fail! You must do this little favour for me."

"I would never get away with it. For one thing, I am taller than Hildebrand."

"Not that much—and you can hunch down a bit if you meet anyone he knows."

"Anyone he knows? Good God, Letty, I should be unmasked in an instant! Suppose I am detected?"

"Never fear," she assured him. "Hildebrand has never been intimate with Lord Ralston's crowd. He is of another generation. Why else would Sir Henry Field be so desirous of his presence?"

"Yes?" Bentley nodded ruefully. "Go on."

"The only other guest of an age with Hildebrand would be Lady Clarissa Langford, for I know she is to be there. But she does not know either of you. Clarissa has become betrothed to Lord Ralston's son, Montrose. I am quite sure Hildebrand does not know him, either."

"And who else am I likely to encounter?"

"No one who knows you, I am certain. We have only to dye your hair; all else is in train. Bentley, we must succeed! My life depends on it!"

"'O what a tangled web we weave—'" he began, but Letitia interrupted.

"No, no! 'Forward, and frolic,'" she declaimed, her spirits miraculously restored as she sensed him weakening. "I, too, have read the poems of Sir Walter Scott. Bentley, only think what a lark it will be, fooling everyone!''

Possibly it was relief at his reprieve, in the form of a prospective heir for the title of Denville, that rendered Bentley temporarily light-headed. He tried on the moustache, studying the effect in the mirror. Truly, if one did not look too closely...

''On your head be it.'' He threw up his hands, admitting he was no match for Letitia's persuasiveness. Actually, he had begun to feel a sneaking exhilaration at the thought of launching into such a masquerade, discovering in himself a latent spirit of reckless daring. It shouldn't surprise him, he reflected. After all, was he not brother to the infamous Hildebrand? He had wondered when he was younger what it would be like to be a devil-may-care, care-for-nobody like Hildebrand. Wondered what it would be like to actually *be* Hildebrand, even for a day.... Now he had a chance to find out.

''You may easily impersonate Hildebrand,'' Letitia was caroling happily. ''He has become a veritable pattern-card of rectitude since our marriage. You have only to be your natural self and no one will suspect our subterfuge.''

This last sent him on his way somewhat reassured but still prey to massive misgivings. To go to Branleigh... masquerading as Hildebrand... and wearing that moustache? He shoved the distasteful object deep into a pocket. He supposed he'd have to, but the hair dye must wash out!

There was, after all, a limit.

CHAPTER TWO

MISS VIOLET LANGFORD wended her way homeward, floating in an impossible day-dream. A few words from a recently read poem fluttered in her mind: "of ruddy limbs and flaming hair." Certainly out of context, yet they seemed somehow apt. The Honourable Bentley Frome was rapidly taking on the aspect of a knight in shining armour. He had not exactly ridden up on a splendid charger and carried her off over his saddle-bow, but one couldn't have everything, even in a day-dream. Besides, her logical side asserted, it would have been decidedly uncomfortable.

But that brief encounter would be enough to fill many a lonely hour. At least she had the memory of her romantic rescue—though she would have preferred to have seen the face of her knight more clearly. Would she ever have another chance? she wondered. Perhaps while walking in the Park with Clarissa, or at one of her parties...

Now, really! Such a man would never attempt to renew his acquaintance with a dowdy spinster! She had best put him from her thoughts. She shrugged delicate shoulders beneath her unfashionable brown merino walking gown. But she couldn't stop bamming herself with nonsensical day-dreams—and she didn't want to. Irksome reality should not be allowed to spoil her private imaginings!

Her pace slowed as she approached the town house of the Marquis of Scofield, Lady Clarissa's father. Surely that was Sir Edward Moore running down the steps and heading off along the pavement away from her. He must have been visiting Clarissa. Had she bade him a final farewell now that she was betrothed to another? Violet's tender heart, easily wrung by lovers parted, went out to him in a rush of sympathy. It might be true that "hopeless love finds comfort in despair," but that seemed a sad solution to her.

She sent a scorching mental message of indignation in the direction of Branleigh, the home of Hippolyta, Dowager Countess of Ralston. If only the beastly female had not taken it into her head to arrange a marriage between her godchild, Clarissa, and her great-nephew, Montrose! And only, Violet was certain, because Clarissa was an heiress, not from any desire to join the two families. Lady Hippolyta had not laid eyes on Clarissa since, at the age of five, her cousin had upset a tea-table replete with sticky jam tarts all over her godmother's Aubusson carpet. The incident apparently had increased Lady Hippolyta's deep-seated dislike of the infantry, for it lasted until both great-nephew and godchild were grown.

With a sympathetic heart, Violet followed the progress of the unfortunate Sir Edward as he proceeded up Grosvenor Street. Accustomed because of her near-sightedness to identifying people by their walk, not by their faces, she suddenly realized something was wrong. That was no despondent set to his broad shoulders. The man looked actually jaunty! Could she have been mistaken in the character of his feelings for her beloved Clarissa?

Quickening her steps, she hurried up to the entrance and waited impatiently for Jobson to answer her knock. She was quite prepared to find dear Clarissa in a bout of hysteria, and frantically searched her mind for phrases of consolation. She fairly ran upstairs to the ladies' withdrawing room where she had left her cousin, curled in the wing-chair before the hearth, deep in the vicissitudes of the heroine in Mrs. Radcliffe's latest novel.

To her surprise, Lady Clarissa now paced the floor, her cheeks pink with suppressed excitement and her fair curls tossing.

She pounced on Violet the moment she reached the door and pulled her over to the sofa, her finger to her lips.

"Violet," she whispered. "I am *not* going to marry Montrose!"

Violet sat up straight. "Clarissa! You mean to cry off?"

Clarissa giggled. "Of course not," she announced sunnily. "I shan't say anything. I shall merely elope with Edward, my very own true love."

"You cannot! Clarissa, it is not at all the thing!" Violet caught Clarissa's hands earnestly. "Only think of the scandal you will bring upon yourself!"

"Not the thing! Why, Sally Jersey herself married Lord Jersey at Gretna Green, and her parents were wed there before her! She could not cancel my voucher for Almack's on so paltry an excuse."

"Almack's! That would be the least of your humiliations."

Clarissa stuck out her lower lip in a charmingly petulant pout and yanked her hands away. "I care not a button for what a lot of gossipy tattle-mongers may say. I love Edward and he loves me, and that is enough for both of us." She rose, posing dramatically.

Aye. 'All for love' would be romantic Clarissa's way. And why not? Violet wondered. To be so loved by a man—to let all the world go by—was that not a favourite dream of her own? But *she* had no social position to lose!

"Clarissa, do but think! The ton—"

"My love, I *have* thought, and Edward and I agree that we cannot let a high-handed old despot ruin our lives."

"Oh, dear."

Clarissa plumped herself down on the sofa once more. "It was my godmother who arranged this odious marriage! Montrose only came to offer for me at her instigation. He is terrified of his great-aunt. As a matter of fact, so is my father, which is why he accepted Montrose's offer without consulting me. Not that I really blame him, I suppose." She nibbled on one slim pink finger. "No, it was not all Papa's fault. I can see how it came about. As a child I had an absolute horror of her, envisaging her as the dragon poor

St. George had to defeat. I was sure she could breathe fire if only she tried.''

Violet sprang up from the sofa and began scurrying about the room, picking up pillows and peering behind the vases on the tables, and Clarissa frowned.

"Do alight somewhere, Violet. I wish to talk to you very seriously."

"In a minute. I have to find my spectacles. Truly, I cannot think without them."

"Oh, they are right here. You must have left them in the chair, for after you went out I found I had been sitting on them all the while."

With a tiny cry of relief, Violet grasped her precious eyeglasses and looked them over for damage. She carefully straightened the bent ear-wires and put them on, settling the gold frame securely over her small straight nose. Facing her rebellious cousin again, she discovered the situation to be more dire than she had feared. Never had she seen the frivolous Clarissa look more determined. She sank back down on the sofa.

Clarissa caught her hands. "It is the only way, Violet. Edward and I must elope, for although Montrose doesn't wish this marriage any more than I do, he insists on going through with it."

"You will be labelled a jilt! On top of being utterly ruined!"

"It cannot be helped. If only Montrose would be reasonable we might between us call it off, but he will not. You see, he does not come into his fortune until he is either thirty-five or marries to please his great-aunt. The old lord thought Monty a spendthrift, so he must subsist on a paltry allowance for nearly ten more years unless he marries me.''

Violet made one last effort to save Clarissa from the total destruction of her reputation. ''Surely there must be some other way than a disastrous journey to Gretna Green! You are sacrificing all!''

''Yes!'' Clarissa beamed. ''Is it not the most romantic thing you've ever dreamed of?''

''It is the road to ruin!''

''No, it is not, for Edward is even now buying himself a pair of colours. Once we are wed, we go to the Continent to follow the drum. He will become a general or a field marshal in a year or two and we shall return in triumph!''

Violet shook her head. ''Oh, Clarissa. Think, my love. The war is over.''

Clarissa ignored this minor detail. She bounced up. Taking a noble stance, not unlike a sea captain announcing his intention of going down with his ship, she raised an imperious hand. ''Do not try to talk us out of it. We have made our decision. Edward and I join our fortunes forever in two days' time. And you, dearest Violet—'' here she delivered a broadside in the semblance of an accolade ''—you, Violet, will be the one to make it all possible.''

Violet squeaked. ''Me?''

Clarissa pounced down on the sofa beside her once more, again seizing both her hands. Her eyes sparkled in a way that made Violet shrink with dismay.

"Yes, you, my dearest friend. Only listen, I have planned all."

"But—"

"Now." Clarissa settled herself comfortably. "First, we are lucky in that my father will be gone from home a week or more. He is raising some question in the House of Lords and then continuing on to Yorkshire. This may not seem to you so great a stroke of fortune until you hear the rest. My godmother has invited me to Branleigh. They are holding some sort of house party for the race meets. This means I shall have to go without him and be under Lady Hippolyta's chaperonage, but she has not seen me since I was a small child. Do you not see? The way is clear!"

"You will start for Branleigh, but meet Sir Edward on the road?"

"No, no! The chase would be on the very moment I failed to arrive. I must appear to be present for at least three days, for we need a generous start to make our escape to Scotland. *You* will go to Branleigh, saying you are me, and no one will suspect!"

Violet shook her head firmly. "No. Someone would detect such a masquerade at once!"

"How? No one there is acquainted with either of us."

"No one but your jilted fiancé. Surely Montrose will be among those present in his own home."

Clarissa shrugged a shoulder. "Montrose will go along with the deception, for I will tell him to do so. Besides," she favoured Violet with a sly, sidelong glance, "I suspect he has a tendre for you. You are the one he should marry. I have seen the way he looks at you when he visits me.''

A warm flush crept over Violet's cheeks. ''Oh, no. You are mistaken. He has never so much as—''

Clarissa brushed her protest aside. ''It is only that you have no dowry. Be that as it may, I am positive he will not expose you. He is no more in love with me than I am with him. He can find another heiress to wed and so please his great-aunt. My godmother is the only villain in this case, and with your help we shall foil her.''

Another objection had occurred to Violet. ''Poor Montrose! I fear Lady Hippolyta will hold him responsible for your flight.''

Clarissa had the grace to attempt a contrite expression. ''I am truly sorry for Montrose, having to face the dragon, but perhaps he can go on a Grand Tour of the Continent for a few years now that Napoleon seems to be contained. I cannot have both our lives ruined.''

Meaning her own and Edward's, Violet surmised. Clarissa cared not a fig for what might happen to Montrose. Or for the pickle Violet might find herself in…. ''What am I to say to Lady Hippolyta to end this charade?''

''Why, nothing at all. You have only to become ill after three days and ask to be taken home. And do not fear that anyone will tumble to our lark, for my loyal Simpson will accompany you. She has been with me forever, as you well know, and can put you right on any problem that may arise.''

At the thought of being backed by the doughty Simpson, Violet almost acquiesced. "But, Clarissa, I have not the gowns to appear at such a function! I should never be accepted."

"You shall wear mine, the very best I have. We are much of a size, and Simpy can pin and tuck wherever is needed. Oh, Violet, think how much fun you will have! Dinners, parties, the race meets! Why, almost I wish I would be there."

"Will Simpson actually condone this...this fatal start of yours?"

Clarissa leaned back on a cushion, satisfied as a purring kitten. "Of course. She adores Edward and will do anything to make him happy. As soon as you leave Branleigh, she will go to Paris, for I have given her the wherewithal to put up at a pension there until Edward and I arrive. Meanwhile, I cannot leave her here to be browbeaten by Papa and perhaps forced to tell where I have gone. That is why she must go with you."

Violet could see nothing ahead but devastation, but Simpson would be with her. . . .

Jobson entered the room and announced the arrival of Montrose.

"Now what can he want?" Clarissa demanded, while Violet hastily removed her spectacles and tucked them into the reticule that had hung, forgot, from her wrist since she returned.

He came in with the mincing steps of a Pink of the ton. Violet, remembering Clarissa's interesting revelation, looked him over with new eyes as soon as he came close enough for her to see. Unlike her molester who had worn the fatal beehive hat, Montrose wore a ridiculously high-crowned beaver, and his coat, of exaggerated cut, was not blue but bottle-green to match the pattern of vines embroidered on his waistcoat. His collar points were so high and stiffly starched that he could not turn his head as he bowed over Clarissa's hand and then her own. She noted with amusement that his gleaming Hessians were adorned with gold tassels, which bobbed when he walked. Violet had a sneaking sympathy for the timid Montrose and excused his dandyism, having realized it was a brave front put on to confound the top-lofty *beau monde*.

Montrose had been a frequent visitor since his domineering great-aunt had sent him to call on the Marquis of Scofield to offer for her god-daughter. Both girls knew him well, and in their company he no longer stood upon his dignity. It soon became apparent that he was bursting with news.

"Do stop waffling," Clarissa commanded. "And be seated. Out with it at once!"

Warm colour flushed Montrose's cheeks and the tip of his nose wrinkled, reminding Violet of an eager rabbit scenting a leaf of lettuce. He perched on a chair and licked his lips. "I collect you have both heard of the Denville diamond brooch."

Clarissa sniffed. "Well, of course we have. It belongs to my friend, Lady Letitia."

"Not any more." He settled back in his chair expectantly. He was not disappointed. Violet merely stared, but Clarissa peppered him with questions until he held up both hands. "I thought you wanted me to tell you."

"Well, do so, then!"

"All right. It seems your friend has been dipping rather deep and has run up some large debts. M'father always has an eye for the main chance, so he bought up her vowels and demanded the diamond in payment, on threat of exposing her to her husband. There was naught she could do but turn the brooch over to him!"

Clarissa gasped. "How could he! Never have I heard anything so cruel! Hildebrand will murder her when he finds out she has been gaming, after he forbade her to even think of it again!"

A smug expression spread over Montrose's weak features. "M'father won't have the gem much longer. I mean to steal it from him and sell it for a fabulous price. Then *let* the old lady hold on to my fortune. It will make no difference to me."

Now Violet gasped and rose to her feet. "You cannot steal from your father!"

Montrose looked a trifle sheepish. "I don't suppose I'd really steal it, but I certainly shall hold it for ransom. Once I have it safe, I shall demand that he make his aunt release my inheritance at once, and then I won't have to wed you, Clarissa. I know that will please you. Indeed," he blushed again and cast a most speaking glance at Violet, "I would be free to marry where I wish."

"Oh!" Clarissa jumped up, clapping her hands. "The very thing! Montrose, I had no idea you could be so clever!'' She whirled to hug Violet and kissed her cheek. "I am certain Violet would not object if you were to marry where you wish."

Violet sat down suddenly, absorbing this new idea. Once she aided Clarissa to elope with Edward, she'd no longer have a home with the Marquis of Scofield. And she was quite fond of the gentle Montrose, who'd make a most biddable husband. Why should she not marry him? Certainly, she'd never have another such opportunity. She knew a moment's hesitation, then cast her doubt aside. It was highly unlikely she would ever again meet her red-headed knight in shining armour, and far more unlikely that he'd offer for her if he did.

Clarissa's voice, pregnant with doubt, broke into her thoughts. "Montrose, you are a dear, an excellent conversationalist and a delight in the dance, but I have no faith in your ability to carry off this scheme. You are a born bumbler and could never steal anything without being caught."

She began to walk back and forth before him, her chin in one hand and a gleam in her lovely eyes. Violet had a sudden premonition. Now what had Clarissa in mind?

"It is indeed fortunate," that devious maiden went on at last, "that I have always been gifted with great cleverness. No, do not speak," she added as Montrose opened his mouth. "You do not yet know of the amazing plot Violet and I have formulated this morning. Only listen." She sank into a chair beside him and proceeded to outline Violet's part in her planned elopement. "Do you see, she will be at Branleigh and able to lend you a hand. You have only to be seen accepting her as me and all will go merry as a marriage bell—except, of course, that that wedding bell will not ring for us."

"No, indeed!" Montrose had paled to a delicate yellow-green. "My God, I shall be dead! Have you any idea of what will happen to me at the hands of my great-aunt Hippolyta when she learns the truth?"

"But she will never know," Clarissa soothed. "I have it all worked out. Violet will simply disappear from Branleigh at night, with no word to anyone. When the news of my elopement arrives, Lady Hippolyta will believe I departed from under her roof, and she will never speak to me again. You must act as though you are devastated." She considered him critically. "Yes, indeed, you are doing it just right. Only look as you do now and she will be convinced."

Violet, recovering from her first shock at being included in a scheme to rob her unsuspecting—and already duped—host, almost giggled at Montrose's open-mouthed horror. Really, she thought, he was well out of this betrothal. He must already be realizing that dear Clarissa could be a younger edition of his formidable great-aunt.

"But—but—" he stammered. "She will know! She always knows!"

It was all Clarissa could do to bring him up to the mark. "Buck up, Montrose," she urged. "You will have the diamond in your possession by the time Violet vanishes, and you will be in command. Only think, you will have your father under your thumb!''

Montrose gazed at her with the hopeless eyes of a hound about to receive a bath, and Violet took pity on him.

''It seems to me,'' she said, throwing caution to the winds ''that if this wild deception is to succeed, it would be best if it were I who steals—that is, obtains—the brooch, after Montrose points out its location. No suspicion could fall on me, for as Clarissa, I would not know of its presence at Branleigh. And I mean to leave at once, in any case.'' She patted Montrose on the head, uncertain of what else to do as he now knelt before her, kissing the hem of her skirt.

Clarissa squealed with delight. ''Oh, Violet, I *knew* we could count on you!''

''There is one condition,'' Violet qualified. ''I will do my best, only if Montrose understands we are merely borrowing the diamond and that he must return it the moment he has his fortune.''

To this the young man agreed, almost tearfully, and Clarissa enveloped her in a hug.

''My dearest Violet!'' she exclaimed. ''I cannot admire you enough. You are our fortress in time of tribulation. Only fancy your having the courage not only to undertake a daring jewel theft, but to help me defy my fire-breathing dragon!''

Reaction set in. Suddenly appalled at what she now could think of only as her foolhardiness, Violet stared straight ahead, overcome by a feeling of impending doom. A fortress she might be today, but inevitably she was bound to end up a cinder, if not a mere pile of ash.

LADY HIPPOLYTA, Dowager Countess of Ralston, was not actually a dragon but a human being, although there were many in her acquaintance who would call this to question. At the moment, certainly, the latter definition was somewhat in doubt. While she did not for a fact breathe smoke and sear her nephew with an incendiary blast, the effect on Lord Ralston was much the same.

During the life of her late, unlamented husband, whose family trait of timidity Montrose had inherited, Lady Hippolyta had ruled Branleigh with an iron hand. She intended to continue to do so. Owing to the ridiculous terms in which he had couched his will—no doubt a last gesture of defiance—all funds were tied up in a trust handled by the firm of her husband's man of business. The estate paid all reasonable expenses incurred by the running of Branleigh but it specifically allowed no extras to the gentlemen for gaming— or gave her any control.

She had no financial hold over either her husband's nephew, the current Lord Ralston, or Ralston's son Montrose, and she had to rely on sheer power of character to uphold her domination and maintain a position of respect at Branleigh. Luckily, she had lorded it over them both for so many years that her authority remained unquestioned. With vim she got on with the enjoyable task of ringing a rare peal over her current victim.

"You invited *Denville? You?* I've nothing against his little wife but who do you think you are to bring a libertine and rake-hell into my respectable home?"

Lord Ralston fought to retain some semblance of dignity and took refuge in accord. "I realize he is something of a gay dog—"

"No, he isn't. He is a man, not a canine."

Ralston shuffled his feet. "Ah, yes, of course. Be that as it may, I cannot turn them off now. It is too late."

He watched Lady Hippopotamus, as he referred to her when safely out of earshot, girding her loins for battle and he cringed. Why must she raise such a wind when he was already fretting like a fly in a tar box? The very thought of the man being under the same roof while the Denville diamond rested in his possibly illegal possession quite cut up his peace. Enough to send him to his bed with a dose of James's powders! He almost quailed, but rashly screwed up his courage. After all, Sir Henry Field was her nephew. "I invited them because cousin Henry asked me to do so." That will take the wind out of her eye, he thought with a bit of satisfaction, but lightning crackled about his head.

"Henry! That irresponsible young jackanapes!"

Ralston stood his ground. "I thought it would be pleasant for Lady Clarissa and Montrose to have other young people about the place. Damn—dashed—quiet out here in the country."

Lady Hippolyta caught her breath. For some reason her pyrotechnics had failed to burn him to the usual crisp. Ever since Ralston won that confounded diamond, he had been getting too big for his breeches. An uneasy prickle ran up her spine. Was her control slipping? She abhorred the thought of becoming a poor relation, a penniless cipher, tolerated instead of venerated in her own home.

"I daresay he'll march in here as bold as Beauchamp," she blustered. "A paltry fellow, more squeak than wool!"

Ralston began to look ruffled, but answered her more sturdily than ever before in his life. "No, indeed! The man's perfectly respectable these days. You may meet him everywhere. Why, he is Top o' the Trees!"

"No, he isn't. I don't doubt he has both feet on the ground like anyone else. Climbing trees at his age? Fustian!" She spoke with all her old vigour, hiding a definite twinge of anxiety. She searched for a leveller to regain face and spoke in classroom French, a language he had never been able to comprehend.

"*Rira bien qui rira le dernier, mon cher neveu,*" she declared smugly.

To her satisfaction, his mouth gaped as he struggled to remember his schoolboy lessons. He was saved by the entrance of his butler, bearing a missive on a silver salver.

Not lacking in wit, the man took it directly to Lady Hippolyta. "Delivered by hand, my lady."

She broke the seal and read it through. "They're not coming!"

"What? What?" The skies cleared above Lord Ralston and the sun broke through. "The Denvilles?"

The dowager sheathed her claws, allowing only the tips to remain. "I am amazed. The man shows signs of sensibility. He says they cannot attend our affair owing to the delicate condition of his lady. He feels he must remain at her side and sends his regrets."

An audible sigh of relief escaped Lord Ralston, but his aunt frowned. Lost, she mourned. Lost was an agreeable bone of contention she had looked forward to gnawing for weeks to come.

Little did she know fate was about to deliver her an excellent substitute.

CHAPTER THREE

IT TOOK Bentley several days to perfect his disguise, for he had a few problems. Not wishing to include his barber in Letitia's dubious scheme, he had to concoct his own hair dye, finally coming up with a mixture of lampblack and pomade. This concoction, while it flattened his curls into a style not too different from Hildebrand's straighter hair, rubbed off easily and required frequent touching up. Its one advantage was in not being completely waterproof; he had hopes of being able to remove it.

The fact that his brother did not wear spectacles created a major difficulty. Without his trusty eyeglasses, Bentley was inclined to fall over furniture, and he was unable to make out the facial features of anyone at more than five paces. It was the moustache, however, that nearly made him wash his hands of the whole affair. The gum adhesive on its back was old and no longer stuck as fast as he could have wished, giving the dratted thing a tendency to droop on the left side.

On the day of his departure for Branleigh, he presented himself to Letitia for a final inspection. She collapsed in hysterical giggles and developed a case of the hiccoughs.

Bentley, who had confirmed by his mirror that he indeed looked very much like his brother, drew himself up, offended.

"I collect you consider me a figure of fun. Very well, I withdraw. It is all off."

"No, no! Please—p-please, Bentley. You are quite perfect! Almost you might hoax me, except that Hildebrand wears both sides of his moustache on his upper lip and one—h-half of yours is dangling to your chin!"

Bentley pushed the recalcitrant section back into place and pounded her helpfully between the shoulder blades. "It will never work. The confounded thing will fall off right in front of Ralston."

Letitia sobered. "That it must not. I have it, Bent—what you did just now!"

He frowned. "What did I do?"

She pulled him over to the mirror. "When you replaced it. You sort of pressed it back and twirled the end."

"I had to be sure it was all together." He blinked at himself, six inches from the glass.

"Do it again," Letitia ordered. "See, it will be a mannerism you must use for a dashing effect. A cynical smile, a twirl of your moustache and a surreptitious push to keep it on. If you do it constantly, no one will suspect it being a necessity." She watched him practice the gesture in the mirror and nodded approvingly.

He tried it several more times, studying his image. It was a stranger—no, Hildebrand!—who looked back at him. He fingered the moustache again, stirred by an inner excitement at the swashbuckling *bon vivant* who returned his gaze. Which brought to mind another difficulty. Hildebrand was known for his elegance.

"Who will take care of my wardrobe? I cannot bring Beecham."

He had a point. His valet was an old family retainer, inherited from Hildebrand when the latter moved to quarters in Town on gaining his majority. Beecham would never put up with what he'd term an outlandish prank.

Letitia considered and then shook her head. "It is no matter. You will be there only a day and a night."

"I cannot simply pocket your brooch and disappear. Ralston would know exactly where it had gone."

"So you will stay two or three days. You can survive without a valet as long as you do not spill soup on your evening breeches."

"It will seem very odd in me to arrive unattended."

Letitia threw up her hands. "Then you must concoct some story. Your man fell ill or had an accident."

With this, Bentley had to be satisfied.

He set off for Branleigh that afternoon, driving his curricle and a favourite pair of bays. Saner thoughts had prevailed, as they annoyingly do, and while he was not actually quaking in his shining Hessians, he felt distinctly nervous. His spectacles were on his nose, to be certain of finding his way. In his pocket he had the beastly moustache, and in his mind a determination to end this devilish masquerade as soon as possible, and meanwhile, to play least in sight until he could escape.

A growing sense of irritation with Letitia came over him. If she had a grain of proper feeling she would have gone directly to Hildebrand and not pitchforked her innocent brother-in-law into this imbroglio. Hildebrand would have settled it all in a trice.

But was he not as capable as his brother? All his life Bentley had felt inferior to his audacious sibling. Could that be the unconscious reason for his undertaking this mutton-headed exploit? A chance to prove to himself that he was as daring and venturesome as Hildebrand? He had to admit he wasn't. Hildebrand would delight in hoaxing everyone, in playing the fool. Bentley Frome, he feared, would merely *be* the fool.

This would never do. He should ride forth like a gallant knight to the rescue of Letitia—who wasn't even *his* lady, but his brother's. As he drove, he remembered his first act of derring-do. That was a very nice damsel he had rescued the other day. He felt he had acquitted himself rather well, and wondered if he would ever see her again. Violet something. A pretty name, Violet. Suited her.

Others might have considered the lady nondescript, but Bentley had found her soft colouring and musical voice much to his liking. He approved of her smooth brown hair, parted in the centre, with a neat braid coiled over each ear and just showing beneath her dowdy bonnet. Her ready knowledge of his favourite poets intrigued him. Fancy, in this day and age, meeting a female with a mind—one who could top his quotes! She was quite the most agreeable girl he had ever met, but like a blasted idiot he had not obtained her direction. How would he find her again?

Evening had come by the time he reached the gates of Branleigh, and he bolstered his failing nerve with the thought that all would be candle-lit. His disguise might pass. He pressed the abominable moustache to his lip and pulled his curricle up at the entrance, feeling like a gladiator about to enter a den of lions. A groom came running. Bentley turned over his reins and delayed a few more minutes, giving precise instructions as to the care of his bays.

BELOW-STAIRS in the butler's pantry at Branleigh, Mathilda, the second housemaid, peered from the small window conveniently placed so that august personage could keep an eye on the entrance and be on hand to open the great front doors for guests. She had no business being in the butler's holy chamber, but knew she was safe; old Hepworth was in the front hall, admitting the arrivals. Thus it was she who first saw the curricle, painted in the distinctive Frome colours—burgundy body with trim and wheels picked out in yellow—and bearing the Denville crest.

Mathilda eyed it sourly, thinking bitter thoughts. Ten years her Norton had served as footman at Frome while she worked as a parlour-maid. Ten years gone down the gutterspout when Norton was caught out in a bit of petty thievery and sent off to Newgate. She had been lucky to get this post at Branleigh.

But what was Denville doing here? All below-stairs had been apprised by old Hepworth that he and his wife would not be amongst those present. As she watched, a groom came up and took the reins, while a gentleman jumped down on the far side of the drive. She knew that lanky figure in the many-caped driving coat and curly-brimmed beaver. Surely that was the Honourable Bentley Frome! And wearing a black moustache!

Something havy-cavy was afoot. Agog with curiosity, Mathilda scurried up the stairs to the green baize doors at the back of the great hall, where she joined two other girls already watching the arrivals through a crack. The Honourable Bentley had just come in, and as she stared with widened eyes, he took off his hat and revealed not red hair but black.

Certain she had stumbled upon a devious impersonation that could somehow be turned to her advantage, Mathilda strained her ears to catch his words as Lord Ralston came forward to greet him. The newcomer bowed formally with elegance and quiet dignity, a far cry from the careless insouciance with which the arrogant earl greeted everyone up to the Prince Regent himself. Mathilda flattened her nose against the door edge, trying for a better look.

Lord Ralston extended his hand. ''Denville! This is a surprise.''

Then he was posing as Denville! Mathilda pressed her fingers to her lips. But why? Her mind began to whirl with speculation. She knew of the fabulous diamond brooch won by Lord Ralston at piquet. Branleigh had been abuzz with the tale for a week. And she knew of the Denville diamond. Mathilda could add two and two and get more than three. There might be a connection with this masquerade.

For the moment she held her peace, but she determined to send a message to Betty, the upstairs maid at Frome with whom she still corresponded. Betty would know if the Denville diamond was missing. Yes, by the very first post!

IN THE GREAT HALL of Branleigh, a light perspiration stood on Bentley's brow. "A—a surprise, Lord Ralston?"

"Yes, heard you weren't coming. Lady Hippolyta received your note, saying you wouldn't be here owing to your wife's being in a delicate way."

Devil take it, he might have known Letitia would neglect some important detail! Bentley was shaken but he rallied. "It is not for months yet," he assured his host and went on, quite truthfully. "Lady Letitia absolutely insisted that I attend."

"Did she indeed?" Ralston gave him a hard look. Bentley wondered for a frantic moment if he were to be unmasked at once, but the man headed for the drawing-room from which Bentley could hear a steady hum of conversation.

Cleared the first fence, he thought. Now for the hedge and water-ditch! How many people in there knew Hildebrand? He caught a breath of relief when, as far as he could tell without his glasses, the faces that turned towards him showed no recognition. Ralston led him directly across the room towards a mountain of purple, which turned out, as he drew near, to be a turbaned female seated on a sofa.

She extended a hand and he bowed over it gracefully, remembered she was of a past generation and barely brushed her knuckles with his lips.

She snorted. "He's acquired some manners!"

He looked up, finally close enough to see her clearly and staggered a bit in shock as her basilisk stare seemed to burn into his very brain.

"You have nerve," she began loudly, tipping back her head and looking down her hawklike nose at him. "An infernal insolence to enter my house again."

Silence fell in the room and Lord Ralston attempted shushing motions. "Now, Auntie!"

Bentley suddenly underwent a sea-change. If he was going to drown anyway, he'd go in dignity, not with his tail between his legs. After all, Hildebrand would be blamed, not he. He patted the moustache into place and gave it a reckless twirl that almost took it off.

"My apologies, Lady Hippolyta, but I could not resist the chance to be in your charming company once again."

Amazingly, her eye softened. "Humph. You have the gall of a gamecock, I must say. Well, as you're here now, there's no help for it. But don't think I've forgot you. I recall your last visit vividly. You kissed one of my maids."

Her voice carried and everyone in the room turned to stare. Bentley turned scarlet with embarrassment.

"Under the stairs," she went on. "Mary, I think it was. No better than she should be, that girl. Never fear, I shall have Hepworth warn all the maids to keep their distance."

"That will not be necessary, madam," he declared quite truthfully. "I assure you that I am now a different man."

She bent to look closer at his moustached features and he felt the flush drain from his cheeks. Had the dratted thing slipped? "I thought you older," she pronounced.

Bentley said the first thing that came to his agonized mind. "My age has not caught up with me. No doubt owing to an abstemious life." Almost before the words were out of his mouth, he realized his frightful error, but she greeted them with a gale of laughter. Luckily, for if ever he stood in need of liquid courage, it was now.

LADY CLARISSA had gone, smuggled from the house by the faithful Simpson.

Upstairs in her cousin's boudoir, Violet stood before the cheval glass gazing at a minor miracle. "Cinderella," she whispered.

Simpson had attired her in one of Lady Clarissa's travelling gowns, a soft blue ribbed silk, and now held out a sapphire-blue pelisse in lightweight cashmere trimmed with ermine.

Violet's straight brown hair had been cropped and curled in the latest fashion and her spectacles were tucked into a reticule that matched the pelisse, comfortingly close at hand for emergencies. The hazy reflection in the mirror told her that she would think the result amazingly becoming, could she but see it clearly.

She turned impulsively to Simpson, who now checked the curling tong to be sure it had cooled before she packed it into the large trunk that held a breathtaking supply of lovely gowns for every occasion.

"I cannot believe the difference made by curling my hair! Oh, but—" a horrifying thought "—what if I am caught in a shower? All this beauty will disappear!"

Simpson pursed her lips. "Just take care you are not. Remember you are a lady, and will not venture out in inclement weather. No 'fashionable' allows her hair to get wet. Always wear a bonnet and have ready your parasol."

Violet turned back to the mirror. "How dreadfully inconvenient. The weather is so often damp." She turned impulsively to Simpson. "But how am I to travel in Clarissa's carriage? I will be detected at once by the coachman!"

From its silver paper in a hat box, the abigail took out a ravishing concoction of pleated silk with a deep brim and ribbon bows in the same sapphire blue as the pelisse.

Simpson permitted herself a tight-lipped smile. "Here is your answer," she said, carefully adjusting it on Violet's curls. "Keep your head down and a handkerchief to your face as you enter and leave the carriage."

Four hours later, Hepworth the butler ushered her into the large drawing-room at Branleigh. Violet had always been an enterprising girl, ripe for any lark her disapproving vicar father had complained, but her knees trembled as Hepworth's sonorous tones proclaimed, "Lady Clarissa Langford."

She stepped into the room and blinked vaguely at a veritable sea of featureless faces. She longed for her spectacles, then was thankful she could see no one clearly, clinging illogically to the feeling that if she couldn't see them, they could not see her.

A pompous, middle-aged gentleman dressed in snuff-coloured velvet stepped forward and seized the tentative hand she extended.

"Well, well, so this is our little Clarissa, all grown up. Montrose, my boy, look who is come. Our dear Clarissa has arrived."

A familiar figure in an olive-green coat detached itself from the crowd and swam into her limited field of vision. Montrose looked terrified, and for a wild moment Violet feared he would give her away in his fright, but he stood buff.

"C-Clarissa," he stammered.

She took his arm and pinched him, under cover of turning him about. "Monty, dearest, are you not pleased to see me?"

He gulped and Lord Ralston clapped him on the back, making him bite his tongue. He stuck it out, touching the tip with a finger. "Ow!"

His father had already taken Violet's other hand and pulled it through the crook of his arm. "Come, my dear. Lady Hippolyta is anxious to greet you."

Prepared by Clarissa, Violet quite expected to be confronted by a fairy-tale dragon, and so was able to return a gimlet-eyed stare with limpid innocence. The lady's first remark cut some of the ground from beneath her feet.

"I remember you with fair hair."

Violet's mind raced. "It—it has darkened as I grew older."

The dowager gave a satisfied grunt. "That would be it. I have noticed that these golden-haired cherubs often develop into drab females."

Merci du compliment! thought Violet, but so formidable was Lady Hippolyta that she murmured only, "Yes, ma'am."

A dark gentleman with a black moustache standing next to her hostess leaned towards Violet and squinted in a most forward manner, rather as if he knew her.

Like all near-sighted persons, she recognized people by their stance and outline rather than their faces, and it seemed to her that there was something hauntingly familiar about the man.

Lord Ralston noticed her expression. "Oh, have you met Denville, my dear?"

"No, no—that is…" She halted, embarrassed, and addressed the dark man. "My apologies, sir. It is just that you look like someone I once met. Someone else entirely."

The dowager humphed. "That's one in your favour, then. I suppose there's no help for it but to introduce him, though I advise you to keep your distance. He's Denville. And this, young man, is Lady Clarissa Langford. She's betrothed to my great-nephew Montrose, Denville, and don't you forget it."

The man, flushing brick-red, looked quite taken aback, but he bowed over Violet's hand with a grace that again gave her a sense of déjà vu. "Your obedient servant, my lady," he said.

Violet started. The words recalled some others, and her own silent response: *her most charming servant.* If only his hair were red.... But of course this was his brother—his infamous brother. No wonder the two were physically alike.

He looked up from her hand, directly into her face, and started in turn.

"Langford." He repeated the name as if it had suddenly sparked his memory. "My lady, are you acquainted with a Miss Violet Langford?"

Violet's grey eyes went blank with terror for a second before she gained control. Denville did not know her! He couldn't! She steadied her voice and answered almost calmly. "Why, yes. She is my cousin." She grew quite brave. "Have you met her, Lord Denville?"

For a split second *he* seemed frightened. "No, oh no, that is, my brother—my brother spoke of her. They, ah, met the other day."

Violet's heart gave a bound. Her knight had thought enough of the incident to mention her! She gave Denville a brilliant smile, but before she could question him, the butler beat the great dinner gong in the hall.

"Ah, 'The guests are met, the feast is set:'" Denville announced. "'May'st hear the merry din.'"

Violet stared at him. Did quotations run in his family? Then Montrose appeared at her elbow, offering his arm.

"Hah!" Lord Ralston exclaimed. "In good time! I declare I am hungry as a horse."

"You're out of luck, then," remarked the dowager, heaving her bulk from the sofa. "There'll be no oats on my table."

"Ha ha," Ralston said mirthlessly.

The company paraded to the banquet hall, and Ralston took his place at the head of the table, after escorting Lady Hippolyta to the wide armchair at the foot. Montrose was seated beside the dowager, with Violet next to him.

She noted that the moustached Lord Denville sat nearly across from her, beside a rather flamboyant lady with glossy black curls and a daringly low-cut gown of practically transparent cerise gauze.

Perhaps, Violet thought, she could draw him aside after dinner, for she was eager to speak to him of his red-haired brother. At the moment, the cerise-gowned lady monopolized him completely.

The meal began and Violet was bewildered by the sumptuous array of delicacies proffered by the liveried footmen who passed about the table in a continuous procession. *Semelles* of carp, dressed lobster, crab, crayfish and prawns were removed with braised pheasant, quail, roast duckling, *fillets de veau* and larded sweetbreads. She counted upwards of thirty side dishes and pastries; jellies, creams and baskets of strawberries lined the table.

She sipped an excellent *potage à la tortue* and glanced across the expanse of white linen at the intriguing Lord Denville. He seemed to be eating slowly and carefully, and she wondered if he had trouble keeping his moustache out of his soup. She was too nervous to do more than pick at the food on her plate herself, causing Montrose to remark that she had the appetite of a bird.

Lady Hippolyta squelched him at once. "No, she hasn't. Haven't seen her consume a single worm."

Violet dropped her fork.

Montrose lapsed into silence after this, leaving her free to study Lord Denville covertly while his lordship's attention was claimed by the black-haired lady. Wine had flowed steadily during the several removes of the first course, and she watched him with interest. She had heard tales of his hard head, and of his exploits when his head proved less hard than expected.

He seemed to have a habit of constantly touching his moustache and twirling one end. She wrinkled her nose. The conceit of the man! Aware every moment of his silly moustache, when he would probably look better without it!

She gasped as yet another course followed, with baked hams, *côtelettes d'agneau,* a haunch of venison, green goose, French beans, cauliflower, fresh-cut asparagus, peas and oysters stewed in cream. Lord Denville refused this last, and in a lull in the general conversation, his voice carried to her clearly.

"'He was a bold man that first ate an oyster.'"

Violet, familiar with the quotation and its context, choked and attempted to turn her giggle into a cough in her napkin. He looked up and she fancied he attempted to catch her eye with a questioning gaze. If only she had her spectacles so she might be certain!

THE YOUNG LADY across the table put Bentley forcibly in mind of the one he had rescued. That girl had given her name to be Violet—and she had mentioned a cousin Clarissa as he'd escorted her to the lending library. The unusual amount of wine he had drunk no doubt clouded his senses. Of a certainty, cousins often resembled one another.

She was watching him. He could feel her eyes upon him as he tried to listen to the rather *risqué* crim. con. about which the brazen female on his right persisted in telling him. His moustache tickled his nose, and when he brushed it down with one hand, the loose side parted company with his lip and drooped over his mouth. He managed to shove it back in place before anyone noticed, but he realized he couldn't possibly keep this up. The sooner he escaped from Branleigh the better.

Somehow the long meal dragged to an end. The dowager collected the attention of the females present, who rose and trailed off to the drawing-room.

The table was cleared; port and brandy appeared. Bentley's tongue fairly hung out, but he didn't dare drink much more. Already he felt quite tipsy and longed for Hildebrand's hard head. He scrambled to his feet thankfully when Ralston gave the signal to join the ladies.

Walking with great care, he made his way directly across the drawing-room, planning to corner Lady Clarissa. But before he could reach her, he was cornered himself by his voluptuous dinner companion in the embarrassingly transparent cerise gauze. Lady Beatrix Redgrave smiled up into his face, her eyes half-lidded, and her sensuous body brushed disturbingly close to his as she fingered his lapels.

"And I feared this party would be dull, Denville," she murmured for his ears alone. "I will be on the terrace in a quarter of an hour."

Bentley's mouth dropped open and he felt the moustache slip. He touched it hastily into place, and, remembering to be Hildebrand, gave it a jaunty twirl. Unfortunately, she took this as a sign of acquiescence, and winked at him. Devil take Hildebrand and his confounded reputation! Now what was he to do?

"And if by chance you cannot escape," she whispered provocatively, "I shall ask Ralston in which room you have been put."

"No!" Even under his breath, his voice cracked. "I mean—no! That is to say, I shouldn't think our host would be disposed to give you my direction."

Her delicate eyebrows, arched black feathers, rose derisively. "I have never known you to be afraid of a little indiscretion. Never fear, I know just how to go on with Lord Ralston." Smiling, she ran the tip of her tongue along her upper lip. "We shall get together somehow."

She nodded and reached up a hand to pat his cheek. As she moved away, Bentley felt the hair on the back of his neck prickle and he looked past her, directly at Sir Oliver Redgrave, her husband. The man's eyes glittered red with murder.

Good God, what would Hildebrand do? Never mind Hildebrand, he knew what Bentley would do. He turned away hastily and slid out the door to the hall.

But not before he saw Lady Clarissa watching the scene, and he was almost sure her mouth twisted in disgust even though he couldn't see her clearly. Shattered, he leaned against the wall in the shadows by the foot of the great staircase.

Someone was coming down with a light-hearted step. Lord Ralston, and in his hand he carried a flat black box about three inches by four, just the size of a jewel case. As he approached, he tucked it into his coat pocket and gave it a loving pat.

He saw Bentley and their eyes met. For a moment Ralston appeared shaken, then he stared back. Bentley had an odd sensation of a gauntlet thrown down and accepted. Ralston passed on into the drawing-room, and Bentley remained where he was.

In his somewhat befuddled state, he hadn't a doubt that it was Letitia's brooch in the flat black case. And, he realized, Ralston thought Letitia had told her husband all about it and that he—Hildebrand—had come to get it back.

Bentley crossed the hall and let himself out into the night on the opposite side from the terrace where Lady Redgrave even now waited. He roamed about in the shrubbery for some time, making and rejecting plans for retrieving the paste jewel. The tickle beneath his nose annoyed him and he peeled off the moustache. Lucky moustache, forsooth! Look at the mess he was in! He'd probably be murdered by that brazen female's husband.

But he'd had one stroke of luck while wearing it. He'd met Lady Clarissa, and now could find the mysterious young lady he had rescued. Denying that he was in any way superstitious, he put the moustache back on—only because fingering it helped him to think.

He circled back to the building and discovered a bench in the light from the dining-room windows. He sat down and bent his mind to his more pressing problem. Ralston had gone up the stairs and returned carrying the case. That meant he kept it in his rooms somewhere. How to find where his lordship slept.... Could he ask the butler? He got to his feet and took a step forward.

A whoosh of air sounded behind him, followed instantly by an earth-shaking thud, and he leaped around.

A huge terracotta flowerpot containing an anaemic palmetto had half buried itself in the soft soil beside the bench.

Less than a foot from where he'd been sitting a moment before.

CHAPTER FOUR

SUDDENLY SOBERED, Bentley stared down at the shards of the gigantic pot in disbelief, then up at the balcony above him. In the light from the moon he could dimly make out a row of miniature palm trees, with one missing like a gap in a row of teeth. A baluster was broken away from the railing before them.

Could Ralston be so monstrously in the wind that he could not keep up his property? Yet that dinner! No sign of cheeseparing there. But why else, unless he faced desperation, would a man of Ralston's social standing stoop so low as to cheat poor Letitia, even going back on his word to a lady of the peerage? And could this be an attempt to frighten him—Denville—away? With a lightening of his spirits, Bentley considered this new riddle.

He poked at the shattered pot with the toe of his evening shoe and some of his *joie de vivre* left him. If his personal *vivre* was to continue, perhaps he'd better settle this business of Letitia's brooch in a hurry. That palm tree couldn't have fallen by itself. Suddenly, he hadn't a doubt but that it had been pushed, only how could he—or himself in Hildebrand's character—present a peril to Ralston worthy of murder?

Into his mind came the image of Sir Oliver Redgrave and his murderous jealousy. Now there was a likely villain! He glanced up at the balcony again with an uneasy feeling that he was being watched by unseen eyes and went back into the house even more quickly than he had left. Better to face a gaggle of females than to remain a target for a potted-palm pusher!

He re-entered the drawing-room, pressing the moustache into place and giving it a securing twirl. Immediately, he was pounced on by a fat and fortyish lady who should not have been wearing low-cut puce satin or a turban of yellow gauze and ostrich plumes.

She simpered coyly. "I can see my name is lost to you, my lord. We met in the hall."

Before he could think of an answer, several more ladies descended on him, their faces vague and blurry. Unused to fending off lures thrown out by shameless females, he panicked. Damn Hildebrand and his reputation, he thought, and so much for playing least in sight! He had been introduced to the entire party and tried frantically to apply titles by the colours of their gowns, but failed.

A pea-green lustring with blond lace trim seized his arm. "Ah, my dear Denville!" she trilled in his ear. "I see you have few acquaintances here. You must allow me to take you under my wing."

She was neatly circumvented by a wine ribbed silk. "Nonsense, Amelia. He has at least one old friend."

Bentley stared at her, horrified. Did she know Hildebrand? A moment later he nearly staggered with relief as she continued.

"I believe my husband is well-known to you, my lord. If he were here he would soon place us on friendly terms, so I see no reason why we should not be so now."

What would Hildebrand do? Rakishly, he twirled the moustache and tried to disengage his other arm. A sharp-featured creature with flashing dark eyes extended jewelled fingers to him, giving him an excuse to pull himself free as he took the hand and bowed over it. She squeezed his fingers, fluttered her eyelashes, and when she walked away, he discovered a twist of paper left in his palm. Uncertain what to do with it, he shoved it into a pocket.

On either side of him, pea-green lustring clashed with wine ribbed silk, and the puce satin joined the fray. The cerise gauze of Lady Redgrave bore down on them and Bentley searched frantically for refuge. He solved the problem by sliding behind a nearby portière. From there he eased his way to the other side of the room and took out the bit of paper.

With a sinking sensation, he read: "Third floor, second door on the right from the landing." He tore the summons to bits and dropped the pieces behind a chair. Turning, he faced a mountain of lavender lace and satin.

"Best thing you could do, Denville," said Lady Hippolyta. "I'll have none of your goings-on under my roof."

"Good God," Bentley gasped. "I wouldn't dream of it!"

The gimlet eyes bored into him and she gave a satisfied grunt. "Dream all you want. Just behave while you're awake."

"Yes, ma'am." He bowed and backed away, only to see Lady Redgrave's husband come into the drawing-room through the French windows.

Lord Redgrave stopped when he saw Bentley, as though surprised. Because Bentley wasn't on the terrace with his wife? Or because he wasn't dead? The thought of a jealous husband pushing potted palms was as fantastic as blaming Ralston. Bentley shook his head in an attempt to clear it of foolish notions. Truly his nerves were as shattered as the terracotta pot. Hildebrand would be ashamed of him.

But Redgrave headed his way purposefully. "Double, double toil and trouble," Bentley thought to himself. Unlike Macbeth, he could still escape. He ducked through a door at the back of the room, found himself in the library and stopped.

Ralston stood by the door to the hall and looked at Bentley with cold eyes.

"If it's a game of piquet you're after, Denville, you are too late." He put a world of meaning in his tone. "If you have come here with some plan to challenge me in an attempt to win back your wife's brooch, you may put it out of your mind. The gaming is over."

Was the rig up? Obviously, Ralston knew why he was here. Bentley raised Hildebrand's second-best quizzing glass, provided by Letitia, and attempted a haughty set-down. He lowered the glass in a hurry. Unlike his spectacles, it turned Ralston's face into a wavering, nauseating blur. How could Hildebrand stand the confounded thing? He hesitated, silently cursing Letitia and her schemes, and said at last, "I have no desire to play games, Lord Ralston."

"Indeed?" His lordship definitely sneered. "You may be sure I do not intend to part with the diamond for the paltry amount of her vowels. Full value of the stone, Denville, and from you a bit more, for I know its importance as an heirloom to your family."

Bentley stared at him, taking offence at such unchivalrous behaviour. By heaven, this settled it. He had come to Branleigh prepared to negotiate, but Letitia had the right of the matter. He would certainly steal the brooch. Ralston had obtained it by foul treachery; by foul treachery he would lose it. "It is a double pleasure to deceive the deceiver."

Bentley squared his shoulders. If he was supposed to be Denville, he'd best start acting like him. He gave the moustache a quick push and a confident twirl.

"If play we must, Ralston, the game is not over. I have not yet shown my hand." He turned on his heel and strode back into the drawing-room. Immediately, puce satin, wine silk and pea-green lustring surged towards him, and he beat a retreat through the nearest French window onto the terrace. He headed for the darkest corner, out of the glow from the flambeaus that lit the garden, and drew a deep breath.

Voices, the female one oddly familiar, drifted up to him, and he looked over the terrace wall. Directly below, seated on a garden bench, were a lady and a dandified young man. Bentley squinted, wishing the flambeau lighting the path was closer. The female wore a blue gown and had soft brown hair. Lady Clarissa? It must be, and the other was Montrose, the son of Lord Ralston, her betrothed.

As he watched, the man caught the lady's hand, kissing it fervently. "My darling," he said. "It is such a relief to say I love you."

Bentley drew back, embarrassed. He abhorred eavesdroppers.

"You are so beautiful in the moonlight," Montrose went on. "Your cheeks are like roses, your teeth like pearls."

"I hope not." The girl giggled, earning high marks from Bentley. "It would not only give me an odd appearance, but I daresay it would be very hard to chew with round teeth."

The young man dropped her hand. "I wish you wouldn't do that. You sound uncomfortably like my great-aunt."

"I'm sorry, Monty, but one of us must be practical."

"Not tonight. Dearest, I have written an ode to you." He rose, and standing before her, he declaimed:

"You walk in beauty, like the night
Of cloudless climes and starry skies;
And all that's best of dark and bright
Meet in your aspect and your eyes."

This was too much for Bentley. He leaned over the wall with a discreet cough. "Very nicely put," he said with a pontifical nod. "One of Byron's best, I believe."

Montrose sprang to his feet. "Who is there?" he demanded.

Shy to the point of diffidence in daylight, Bentley discovered in himself a Hildebrandish self-assurance in the dark shadows. "Pray continue," he begged. "'Tis a night made for poetry and Byron is an excellent choice. 'Such great achievements cannot fail To cast salt upon a woman's tail.'"

"What!"

"Samuel Butler," Bentley explained to him with gentle patience. "*Hudibras,* you know. Quite unexceptionable."

The girl giggled again and Montrose turned to her, his voice quavering with fury. "I think we had best go inside, Vi—that is, Clarissa."

Bentley's heart gave a great bound at this *faux pas.* What, then, was going on? Abruptly, a depressing thought struck him. Could this be Violet and not Clarissa? Violet betrothed to Montrose—and in secret? Committed to a man who hadn't the courage to claim her and so forced her to masquerade as her cousin to be near him? This would not do—not if he could prevent it.

The girl still sat on the bench, staring upwards, and Montrose pulled at her arm. "Come on."

"No, no," said Bentley, resting his elbows on the wall. "Do not leave on my account. I shall remain here, 'silent as the moon,' though 'I had rather be a dog, and bay...'"

VIOLET ALSO REMAINED, making no move to leave. She squinted up, fascinated, at the pale blur hanging over the wall above her. Its only salient feature was a black moustache. Denville! Her pulses began a rapid beat that surprised her, until she realized it was only the startling resemblance of his mode of speech to that of his red-haired brother that intrigued her.

Montrose was pulling at her arm again and she pushed his hand away.."In a minute, Monty. Do you go in. I—I wish to speak to Lord Denville."

The moustached man straightened his lanky frame and strolled down the terrace steps with a graceful elegance that made Monty seem short and awkward.

"You may be sure, sir, that I will see her safely inside," he said as he came up to them.

For a moment Montrose squared up as though to protest, and Violet rose quickly, putting her hand on his arm. "It is all right, Monty. Go, please. I will join you in a few minutes."

He hesitated, looking up at the taller man, who waited courteously. He glanced at her and then, to her relief, stalked back into the house.

The other man started to raise his quizzing glass to inspect Montrose's retreating back but seemed to have second thoughts.

"'O gracious God,'" he remarked. "'How far have we Profan'd thy heavenly gift of poesy!'" He turned to her, shaking his head. "You should not be out here in the garden alone with a man who steals another's words.''

Indignant, Violet flared. "He is my fiancé!"

"Tsk-tsk. You cannot mean it. 'I have seen better faces in my time Than stand on any shoulder that I see Before me at this instant.'"

"You do not see him. You have chased him away."

"No, no." The moustache turned back to her. "That was your doing, not mine. Nor do I blame you—he is not good enough for you."

"Indeed! And who are you to belittle him? Montrose is a respectable gentleman and you—you... He has not a reputation such as yours!"

She could not see his grin, but she heard it in his voice.

"My, my, 'Though she be but little, she is fierce.'"

Violet, irrationally, giggled. "I collect, like the lion, I am 'not so fierce as painted.'"

"Lion...lion..." He gazed down the dark path. "Ah, I have it. This night was not made for quarrels. 'Let bears and lions growl and fight.'"

"'For 'tis their nature, too.'" She finished the quote triumphantly.

He chuckled with delight. "My girl, you are priceless."

Violet realized suddenly that she was not behaving at all as she should. "You were very rude to Montrose, my lord," she said primly. "He went to a great deal of trouble to memorize those lines."

"Another poet, less easily recognized, would have been preferable. Now if I were to borrow a quote for you, here in the moonlight, I should go to Spenser's *Faerie Queene* and say you make me think of 'Roses red and violets blew, And all the sweetest flowres, That in the forest grew.'"

There was a warmth in his tone, and Violet caught her breath, feeling a like warmth flush her cheeks. How could two men, even though brothers, sound so alike? She tried to see his face, but the light from the flambeau was too weak and far away.

"You are very like your brother," she said. "In your manner of speech as well. Do you both habitually lard your conversation with quotations?"

For a moment he seemed to hesitate, then he gave his moustache that rakish twirl. "Playing 'top the quote' has become a contest between us. Believe it or not, I too received a highly expensive education, and Bentley keeps me on my toes. In your case, however," he went on, "there is no need for poetry. 'To throw a perfume on the violet... Is wasteful and ridiculous excess.'"

Violet gasped again. Twice he had mentioned that flower. But he couldn't know—or could he? Suppose he knew the real Clarissa! And whether he did or not, he should not be speaking so to her in a dark rose garden.

"I—I am a friend of your wife's," she reminded him, a challenge in her words. Now what would he say?

But he was not fazed. "Are you, my lady? Yes, I believe I have heard her mention your name."

She sank onto the bench, her knees giving way. He did not know Clarissa. Her secret was safe for the nonce, but the sooner she borrowed that diamond brooch for Montrose the better. Even to herself she did not add that the sooner she put a distance between herself and this intriguing—and married!—man, the happier she would be. She was far too aware of a sense of rapport between them, and deep inside, it bred a niggling fear. To put it to flight, she spoke aloud.

"I am betrothed to Montrose."

"Who knows 'What next morn's sun may bring,'" he murmured, as though to himself.

She looked up, startled. "I beg your pardon?"

"Naught. Mere maundering."

He was interrupted by a vigorous "Halloo!" in a strident female voice, followed by, "Montrose? Lady Clarissa?"

Violet started to her feet, but was pushed back by a gentle hand on her shoulder.

"I fear," he remarked, "Lady Hippolyta is hard on your trail."

And she must not be caught! Of all things, to be found in the moonlit garden with a man of Denville's ilk—she would be ruined! Violet shrank back into the shadows against the wall, out of reach from the light of the nearest flambeau.

The moustached gentleman stepped out into the path. "She's gone along the terrace," he said under his breath. "I believe we are undetected. What a truly formidable dame!"

Violet stifled a rising giggle. "Monty told me he calls her Lady Hippo—when out of her earshot, of course."

"Oh, definitely, of course. I daresay the man cannot be bad on all points. I concede him the gift of coining the apt epithet in this case. She has 'an unforgiving eye, and a damned—' pardon me '—disinheriting countenance.' Avoid her, my girl; at close hand she has the look of a basilisk."

"She—she is my godmother." For Clarissa's sake, Violet felt she should play her part and defend the lady. But Lady Hippolyta's very nearness had her quaking. "Is she gone?"

"Aye. 'All, all are gone, the old familiar faces.' That is, she's gone to the other end of the terrace."

Violet stood up. "Then I suggest we be gone also, before she comes back. 'He who flees, will fight again!'"

"Indeed, 'Let us fly and save our bacon.'"

She stopped, alive with interest. "Wherever had you that?"

"Oh, sorry. Rabelais. I trust he has not been included in your education, but it would be advisable to take these words of his to heart."

He took her hand, leading her towards a door at the opposite end of the terrace. His grip was firm and warm, and Violet found herself accepting it all too willingly.

They entered a darkened room and were feeling their way through a jungle of furniture when Lord Ralston's voice, raised in anger, sounded from a closed door on their left. Montrose's answering bleat brought them to a halt. The words between father and son were indistinguishable through the thick panelling, but that they quarrelled was evident.

"Verily, 'a knock-down argument,'" Violet whispered.

The man beside her thought a moment. "'Tis but a word and a blow.'"

"Oh, but 'The blast of war blows in our ears,'" she triumphed.

An arm went about her shoulders, giving her a quick hug and shocking her to silence.

"My dear girl," he whispered. "I say it again, you are a treasure! Do not, I pray, throw yourself away on that puling nodcock."

Shaken by the sensation of comfort—and rightness!—in that light embrace, Violet clung to a chair back her groping hand discovered before her. She tingled with awareness of the tall figure beside her in the dark room. Oh, she must not! Her every nerve signalled urgent warnings. She had to leave Branleigh at once—and get far, far away from the dangerous Lord Denville. So this was why she had been told to steer clear of a rake! Not because of physical peril, but to save her vulnerable heart!

But she couldn't leave yet. She had promised Clarissa three days' grace to see her and her Edward well on their way to Scotland, and she'd promised Montrose she'd help him borrow that . . . that dratted diamond.

And she was wasting valuable time. Lord Ralston was downstairs, and if his argument with Montrose continued, this was an excellent chance for her to make a quick search of his room. She knew where it was, for her own room was next to those of Lady Hippo—Hippolyta—and the master's suite was across the hall at the front of the manor.

She withdrew a hand that somehow was being held by her companion and fled across the darkened room, making all speed.

BENTLEY SWORE QUIETLY to himself. Devil take it, he had frightened her. Naturally, she'd be wary of any advances from a man of Hildebrand's reputation— and she believed him to be married! He swore again, this time aloud, and became aware of silence in the other room. Ralston and Montrose must have gone. Bentley let himself out into the hall cautiously, checking first through a crack in the door to make sure he was unobserved.

Violet had disappeared, and he had only a glimpse of Montrose as that gentleman walked into the drawing-room, where the other guests still milled about. He had no desire to join them. Even at this distance he caught flickering bits of pea-green, cerise, puce and wine among the gentlemen's dark coats, and he shuddered. A vision of his room upstairs presented a haven, and he was looking about for a way to bypass the hazardous salon when he heard a door open near at hand.

Ralston came out, his back to Bentley, and headed with an air of purpose down the hall. On an impulse, Bentley followed him quietly. He had no idea where Ralston's rooms were located, but even if that was not where the man was going, a little spying out of the ground would not come amiss.

He was in luck. Ralston led him to the great hall and the main staircase. Bentley waited until the man rounded the first landing and then ran lightly after him. Above-stairs, the halls were nearly dark, lit only by sconces at long intervals, but he could see Ralston ahead of him, climbing one more flight. The man must be going to his bedchamber, a perfect time for a quick reconnaissance.

The long corridor and wide landing were dotted with odd chests, tables and ancient carved benches. Bentley crouched behind an oaken stand holding a huge vase of Oriental design and watched Ralston walk down the hall. Without his spectacles, Bentley knew he would not be able to see which door, if any, the man entered. He got to his feet, inadvertently bumbling into the stand. The gigantic vase rocked.

He caught it with both hands, steadied it and set it back in place, perspiration dampening his brow. The confounded thing was probably Ralston's pride and joy, and the man would not be happy if he dropped it. On closer inspection, he decided it might have been better if he had. Definitely, it was not Ming. Even in the dim light from a nearby sconce, its decoration was regrettable.

But he had taken his eyes from Ralston, and in those few moments, his quarry had vanished.

Bentley continued on down the hall, pausing at the next intersection uncertainly. Had Ralston gone into one of the rooms he had passed? Or had he gone on ahead?

As he stood, undecided, he heard a rustling sound behind him. But before he could turn he was struck a shattering blow on the back of the head. His last memory was of the pattern on the floor carpeting rising slowly up to meet him.

ALMOST DIRECTLY ABOVE HIM, in her attic room, Mathilda the housemaid gripped a worn quill. The tip of her tongue protruded from between her thin lips as she grappled with the erratic spelling of the King's English. The second footman, being sent into London on the morrow, had promised to deliver her missive in person to Betty, the upstairs maid at Frome House. He would wait for her answer.

CHAPTER FIVE

A DEVILISH THROBBING in his head woke Bentley. The
bed on which he lay was uncommonly hard, but it was
too much of an effort to open his eyes and see where
he was.

Gradually he became conscious of something on his
face, tickling his nose. He brushed at it—then dashed
it away, wide-eyed with horror. A furry caterpillar! He
tried to rise and fell back, striking his aching head a
nasty whack on what he now perceived to be a car-
peted floor. He clutched his temples, trying to focus
his vision through a whirl of sparkling lights, and lay
still. His head cleared at last, with startling sudden-
ness.

Candles in a sconce above his head disclosed a hall-
way, a hall in Branleigh. Someone had hit him over the
head…he was pretending to be Hildebrand…and that
caterpillar was his Denville moustache! He pawed
about on the carpet beside him until his questing fingers touched the repulsive scrap of black hair. His
weakened intellect strained to discover which side of
it went up, and minutes went by before he secured it
properly in place. He continued to lie flat, exhausted
by the effort. Closing his eyes seemed to help.

A nearby door creaked as it opened in a tentative fashion, and he tensed. Then light footsteps ran to his side.

"Oh, dear, is that you, my Lord Denville? What has happened?" A feminine voice, tight with anxiety...

He felt a cool hand on his pounding brow and looked up into Violet's frightened face. His first thought was to reassure her. "I'm all right." He tried to sit up and groaned in spite of himself as a stab of pain shot through his head.

"No, no, do not try to rise." She pressed him back down. "Only tell me what happened."

Bentley's splitting ache began to localize and he touched a rising goose-egg behind his left ear. "It would seem that someone doesn't approve of me. I appear to have been struck down. Not by an expert, fortunately—it was a glancing blow."

She was kneeling at his side, and now started to get to her feet. "Lie quiet, my lord. I shall bring help."

He caught at her skirts. "Good God, no. I'll be all right in a few minutes." The last thing he wanted was to be found here, so close to Ralston's rooms. His own apartment was in another wing. But just a little while more...lying at her feet with her soothing hand on his forehead...she looked so worried, and so sweet. He knew a sudden urge to tell her that he knew her for Violet and to unmask—or unmoustache—himself. A veritable ministering angel, that was she. In his present weakened state he was unable to prevent himself from quoting the all too familiar lines from Marmion.

"'O Woman!'" he began. "'O Woman! in our hours of ease, Uncertain...'"

"Yes, yes," she said hastily. "Never mind that now. Are you badly hurt?"

"No." He struggled to a sitting position, steadying his head with both hands. "Thank God you stopped me. I might have spouted the entire dratted verse."

She sat back, relieved. "Ah, I see you are once more yourself. Who did this to you?"

"I have no idea." Bentley looked about vaguely. The pseudo-Ming vase lay in splintered shards about them. It could not have been Ralston, he thought. Not with what the man may have believed to be a treasured *objet d'art*. "At least that hideous vase is no more," he said. "Truly, it is 'an ill winde that bloweth no man good.'"

Violet giggled. "If you are indeed better, I feel we'd best quit this spot before we are seen and I am totally compromised. I hear someone coming up the stairs."

She spoke too late. Already, the hefty form of Lady Hippolyta had reached the landing, and she came stumping towards them. They stared at her in frozen silence. Like a loaded barge labouring up the Thames, she drew up and came to anchor. She looked down at Bentley, who hurriedly pressed at his moustache and gave it a hard twirl. Her gaze transferred to Violet and then took in the shattered vase. She nodded approval.

"An excellent device, my child," she said to Violet. "That should discourage the most persistent rake." Obviously she had jumped to the conclusion that the girl had been forced to a desperate measure to protect her virtue. For some reason—perhaps the same reason—neither of them felt called upon to disabuse Lady Hippolyta of that belief.

"Go to your room, girl," she ordered. "I have a few things to say to Denville. And if you need to go out again at night, use the chamber-pot."

Blushing furiously, Violet ran across the hall and into her bedroom. The door slammed behind her.

"I don't suppose, Denville," Lady Hippolyta remarked as Bentley slowly clambered to his feet, "that anything I could say would do a bit of good to one as ramshackle as yourself. Suffice it to say that I mean to keep you under surveillance." She fixed him with a belligerent eye, but his head spun so badly that her admonitory gaze had no effect.

She frowned. "I daresay you are in no condition to retaliate, so I shall not waste my words. Lady Clarissa is no flibbertigibbet to be taken in by the likes of you. Not at all the pretty widgeon I expected from the reports I've received from friends in Town. She shows great sense. See that you keep your distance!"

That, Bentley could easily swear to do, and he did so. He had no intention of meeting the real Clarissa.

Lady Hippolyta nodded in satisfaction. "She's too good for my gap-witted nephew, but she's not a conquest for you, either. I suggest you return to your own room at once. Vinegar-soaked brown paper applied to the brow," she suggested in a milder tone. "Or half a cup of strong tea with a shot of whiskey and some honey in it. Call on Hepworth; he'll know what's best for a headache."

LADY HIPPOLYTA turned away ponderously and left Bentley standing in the hall, for all at once she had some serious thinking to do. Somehow she doubted that Denville had pursued Clarissa to her room. For one thing, she had caught sight of the girl slipping up the main staircase nearly half an hour before. From the drawing-room, she had seen Denville look in some time later and then take flight—not that she blamed him. Her rouged lips twisted in a malicious smile. Served the man right to get a taste of his own medicine. She had quite enjoyed watching him flee from those idiotic females. But what had caused him to flee into this wing of the house?

She let herself into her own chambers. Denville had no business over here. She had taken particular care to place him in a room at the other end of Branleigh, as far as possible from Montrose's fiancée. There was only one thing that would draw him to this vicinity— the Denville diamond. Even as she thought it was a possibility, she became certain. He had come for Lady Letitia's diamond brooch.

She dropped onto the side of her bed, sinking the feather mattress down to the creaking ropes that supported it. Of course! Ralston must be negotiating to sell it back to Denville. The very idea of her rascally nephew profiting to such a vast extent left a bitter taste in her mouth.

But if Denville intended to buy back the brooch, why was he sneaking about the halls? Lady Hippolyta was no slow-top and she knew a quickening of her pulse. The man meant to steal the stone, not purchase it. And why not? It was rightfully his. It would suit her own purpose well if Ralston were to be separated from that gaudy bit of treasure without gain... but why should she not profit herself? She could use the small fortune the diamond would bring far better than he.

Suppose the brooch were to disappear, who would Ralston suspect? Not herself certainly, not with Denville on the premises. That stone would fetch a pretty penny. She took a deep breath. It was high time the financial reins of Branleigh were safely back in her own hands.

Now where, she wondered, would her blasted nephew be likely to hide that confounded brooch? She resolved to keep an even sharper eye than usual on his perfidious lordship. She had no great opinion of his intelligence. He would give himself away before long. He'd be unable to resist taking out the brooch to gloat over it.

VIOLET HEADED DOWN to breakfast early the next morning, unable to wait longer to discover what had happened the night before. She still shuddered at the recollection of Lord Denville sprawled on the corridor floor in the pool of yellow light from the candle sconce on the wall. The sight of his tall, urbane figure lying pale and vulnerable at her feet clutched at her heart even now.

She had known a wild desire to gather him into her arms, to protect him—so powerful an urge that it frightened her. The man could take care of himself! But a doubt had been seeded within her and now sprouted, a growing fear. Someone had hurt him and might try again . . . he needed her by his side!

But she couldn't be there. Dear God, what was she thinking? To have such feelings for a married man! Every sensibility must revolt. She struggled to regain her composure. Had Denville become so particular in his attentions that the others had noticed? She thought back frantically. Surely not. And after Lady Hippo's interpretation of the scene last night, if the woman had any suspicions they must be laid to rest. Now if only she herself could maintain a proper distance from that dangerous gentleman, and quell her responses to the very sight of him, all might be well. She must not, would not, allow herself to develop a tendre for the wedded Earl of Denville.

When she entered the breakfast room, only Beatrix Redgrave and her husband were present. Violet walked on in, feeling far more secure than the day before at playing the part of her cousin. The faithful Simpson had attired her in one of Clarissa's loveliest morning gowns, a simple round dress in rose-pink muslin with short puffed sleeves and two deep flounces on the skirt.

She felt ready for anything—except the continuing absence of Lord Denville as she slowly ate her breakfast, carrying on a desultory conversation with Lady Redgrave about the weather and the possibility of rain interfering with the next day's trip to the race meet. She didn't realize how eagerly she had looked forward to meeting Lord Denville again until he failed to put in an appearance. Startled by the strength of her disappointment, she did not dare ask where he was.

Not so Lady Redgrave, who this morning wore a daringly masculine riding habit. When she imperiously ordered Hepworth to tell Lord Denville that she had requested two horses from the stable and wished him to ride with her, her husband rose ominously from his chair.

"Oh, sit down, Oliver," she snapped, and he sank back, red-faced.

Hepworth, his nose elevated, relayed her request to a footman, and Violet waited somewhat anxiously for Denville's reply, while Lady Redgrave drummed her fingertips on the table.

The footman returned and whispered to Hepworth.

"Well?" Lady Redgrave demanded.

Hepworth gave her a faint, cold bow. "Lord Denville, my lady, is suffering from a headache and has asked for a tray in his room. He sends his apologies and begs you will excuse him."

Lord Redgrave leaned back in his seat with a sneer. "I'm afraid, my love," he remarked, "you will have to settle for my company."

Beatrix Redgrave threw down her napkin. "I've changed my mind," she said. "I do not feel like riding after all."

Seeing violent storm clouds gathering, Violet excused herself and fled to the quiet library, where she could indulge in her secret delight at Denville's rebuffing the brazen Lady Redgrave.

There was a fire in the hearth. Violet curled up in a wing-chair before the warm blaze and tried seriously to consider her situation. Her attempt the evening before to search Lord Ralston's room had been foiled by a housemaid, who had chosen that inopportune time to turn down his lordship's bed.

The woman had given quite as guilty a start on seeing her as Violet had herself. The maid must have forgot to do the task when she should have and only then remembered it. Well, Violet certainly was not going to mention her being remiss in her duties, and she only prayed the woman would not mention her own arrival at Ralston's room at that late hour.

Violet had retired to her own chamber nearby. She'd waited for the maid to depart, watching at a crack in her door. The maid hurried by almost at once, but just as Violet started out, Ralston himself appeared on the landing and she had to give up. Only minutes later, she heard the crash that culminated in her finding Lord Denville prostrate on the floor, surrounded by the shards of the Oriental vase. At first, she had been vastly puzzled by Denville's presence in the family corridor of Branleigh—her cheeks grew hot as she remembered Lady Hippolyta's conclusion and calm acceptance. She was back in her own bedroom, the door slammed and her back braced against it, before she realized why he was there. The Denville diamond, of course. He would be after it, too!

He must have come to speak privately to Ralston, to buy back the Denville heirloom. But who could have broken that vase over his head? And why? Her heart grew suddenly cold. Surely not Montrose! It was just the muddle-headed sort of thing he would do if he thought the diamond might pass beyond his reach. She'd best speak to him at once. If she was to keep him out of dire trouble, she'd have to steal the brooch herself, and quickly. The first order of business would be to find out where it was kept.

She rose from her chair, determined to locate Lord Ralston immediately. He saved her the trouble by entering the library as if on cue.

He seemed taken aback on finding her in this book room, but being a forthright young lady, Violet seized her advantage.

"My lord! I was just looking for you. We have not yet had a chance to become acquainted."

If he'd had Denville's moustache, she thought with a private smirk, he'd have given it a twirl.

She gave him her most charming smile, all the while striving to recall Clarissa's coy mannerisms. Tucking her hand into his arm, she led him to the chair by the fire.

"Do tell me about Branleigh, and about yourself," she cooed, ducking her head and grimacing to herself. She felt a fool to be acting so missish, but was rewarded by his patting her hand with a far from avuncular air.

"I have been told by Montrose of your powers at piquet," she went on, fluttering her eyelashes. "He tells me you are quite a master of the game."

Ralston transferred his pats to his impeccable neckcloth, actually preening himself. "Why, now that you speak of it, I, ah, believe I do have some small skill at the pasteboards.''

Violet gazed at him, wide-eyed. ''Montrose told me you have won vast sums, even jewels. A huge diamond, I think he said.'' She wondered if she had gone too far, for Ralston seemed a trifle ill at ease. She rushed on. ''How I would love to see such a great stone.'' She tried hard to imitate Clarissa's most coaxing tone. ''Would you—could you let me take just a peek at it sometime?''

Ralston hesitated. He glanced at the door and then down at the most innocent and trusting expression Violet could manage. He capitulated. From an ingenious little cubby-hole stitched into his waistcoat to hold a pocket watch, he took a small packet of wrapped silk. He unfolded it carefully and Violet gasped as she looked at the Denville diamond.

It was the centre-piece of a golden brooch shaped like a nest of ivy leaves, studded here and there with smaller stones and so large that she felt it must be glass.

''It can't be real!'' she exclaimed. ''I have never seen a gem of such size!''

Ralston was already refolding the silk and tucking it back in his watch pocket. ''Oh, it is genuine, all right, and it will bring me a tidy sum.''

''What a shame to let it go out of your family!'' Particularly, she thought, if he sold it back to Denville before she could get it for Montrose. ''You must not sell such a treasure.''

"As for that—" Ralston smiled down into her beseeching face "—I daresay you think it would make an excellent wedding present, eh? Well, well, we shall see." He suddenly looked as though he regretted having shown her the brooch. "You must excuse me, my dear child." He touched the little pocket, making sure of its contents. "Other guests to see to, you know. Where is Montrose? I shall send him to you. I fancy you'd like a tour of your future home, would you not?"

Violet was forced to agree. What she wanted was not Montrose but a chance to think. She considered Lord Ralston with a speculative eye as he left the library. Obtaining that magnificent gem would be more difficult than she expected if he kept it on his person. But would he always? Tentatively, she nibbled a fingertip but stopped as she recalled Clarissa doing the same while she thought up some of her most outrageous schemes. She was becoming entirely too much like her flighty cousin. It would never do to think as Clarissa would. She needed to be practical.

Ralston would not wear that waistcoat to bed, so must have some other place to keep the diamond. He also would not wear it to dinner, for she was sure his evening apparel would have no such pocket. That evening, while the gentlemen sat at their port, she could slip away on some pretext from the ladies in the drawing-room. His bedroom would be empty then, if only that bothersome maid did not decide to come in. It was worth taking the chance.

The door burst open and Montrose bounded through. "Vi—I mean, Clarissa—Father said you wished to see me at once. Do not tell me—I mean, *do* tell me you have found the—" he lowered his voice to a whisper "—the you-know-what!"

"I know where it is, if that is what you mean." She shook her head at his radiant expression. "No, no. It is quite out of our reach as yet, but you'll never guess what he has hinted. He suggested that it might make a suitable wedding gift."

"Glory!" Montrose exclaimed, seizing both her hands. "We shall be wed as soon as I can obtain a special licence!"

"Monty, you are forgetting that I am not Clarissa. He would never consent to our marriage."

"Then we must be wed all the more quickly—now, while you pose as Clarissa. We could be married here in our chapel."

She pulled away. "It would not be legal!"

"Only until he hands over the diamond. Then we may confess all and be married again using your true name."

"Monty, it would never work." But she saw that she'd failed to convince him. "Let me try first to obtain the brooch now that I know where he keeps it. That is, I know where it is part of the time. I have only to discover where he hides it at night."

Montrose's jaw set stubbornly. "I do not see why we should not be wed and claim the stone. There is no need for us to steal it."

"There is every need if you are to gain possession of your funds in a legal manner. Well, almost legal. I will not go through a fictitious marriage. Only think of the scandal should the story come out! Wait, please, and give me a chance to borrow the brooch for you."

He still resembled a baulky mule, and Violet knew a strong misgiving. If only he did not take it into his head to try for the diamond himself, for he'd surely make a hopeless mull of it!

BENTLEY WAS SEATED on the edge of his bed, holding his throbbing head, when the footman arrived with Beatrix Redgrave's summary order. He refused it before he even thought. That Redgrave female terrified him. And not only her—the whole household teemed with predatory females. In his weakened condition, he was in no shape to contend with any side issues.

Between the Redgrave, the potted palm and the Oriental vase, he had a decided feeling that it was time to go home and give up this dangerous masquerade before Ralston—or Lord Redgrave—succeeded in removing him from the premises feet first. If he was going to be murdered, he'd rather die as himself and not as his infamous brother.

But he had promised Letitia. If he failed to obtain her paste diamond before its falsity was discovered, his young sister-in-law would be socially ruined, not to mention what Hildebrand would have to say about her gaming against his strict decree. As a gentleman, he was honour bound to remain at Branleigh. It was beastly inconvenient to be a gentleman. How much better to play the irresponsible rake, as had Hildebrand himself before his redemption through his love for Letitia.

As he sat, awaiting his breakfast tray, his roving eyes settled on the beaver he had worn on his arrival. It rested on its crown to preserve the stylish set of its curly brim, and the inner band was exposed to view. He knew a moment of horror. He was bound to forget some detail, and this surely would have given him away had he not spotted it. The band was so smudged with his home-made hair dye that it looked as though it had been jammed on the head of a chimney-sweep. He had remembered to protect his pillow by wearing a night cap, now hidden in the depth of his valise, but he had never thought of his hat. Devilish lucky, he congratulated himself, that he had not brought a new valet in place of old Beecham.

He dug the jar of lampblack and pomade from its hiding place, wrapped in the nightcap, and scooped out a finger full. The sooner he got away from here the better....

But as he treated the band until it was all the same colour, he experienced a pang of regret. He liked being Hildebrand. Playing the game of "top the quote" with Violet the night before had been stimulating. Never had he encountered a female so well-read. There were so many things he could say to her—and do!—that he never could have as Bentley. Wearing the black moustache seemed to sweep away all his stuffy inhibitions. Donning it was like putting on a whole new personality, becoming someone at once dashing and daring, quite unlike his stodgy self.

He rubbed a finishing touch to the hat-band, realizing as he did so that the action was somehow symbolic. He was committed. He was going to stay. He had made up his mind and he would play out the game, whatever the outcome.

And it wasn't as though he hadn't a clue as to the whereabouts of Letitia's confounded brooch. He had a clear picture in his memory of the black-velvet case Ralston had slipped into his pocket as he came down the stairs. Not that it helped much. But Ralston didn't carry it on his person at all times—witness his going upstairs after it that night. Undoubtedly, he kept it somewhere in his room. Bentley would just have to get into the man's bedchamber and search, and what better time than when the gentlemen sat at their port after dinner. He could easily excuse himself for a call of nature.

In fact, he thought, he might venture out of his room this morning, after his headache let up—and after he was certain Lady Redgrave had gone on her ride. It was all very well to swagger about in a false moustache, but there was no need to tempt fate. He enjoyed playing the role of Hildebrand with Violet, but the masquerade made him quite uncomfortable with any other female and brought trouble upon him from all quarters.

Lady Hippolyta had apparently warned all the housemaids. The girls he encountered when he finally left his room fled when they saw him coming down the hall. Now that he came to think of it, only one house-maid had entered his chamber that morning. The same woman had brought his breakfast tray and his luncheon, and she seemed completely unafraid. Indeed, she seemed unnecessarily zealous, returning to make up his bed, lay a fresh fire in the hearth and generally hover about.

He wondered for a moment if she could be the maid Hildebrand had kissed beneath the staircase five years before, but rejected the thought at once. He distinctly remembered his brother saying that damsel was ravishing, while this female looked more as though she had been ravaged. A number of times. He dismissed her from his mind.

A MISTAKE. The maid Mathilda was worthy of some profound thinking on Bentley's part.

The second footman returned from London in time to serve the evening meal, and he brought Mathilda an answer to her note to Betty, the upstairs maid at Frome House. She unfolded the twist of paper with shaking hands and strove to make out Betty's illegible scrawl.

All her suspicions were confirmed. The butler at Frome had overheard part of Lady Letitia's conversation with her brother-in-law—not enough to know their plans, but sufficient to guess that the Denville diamond was involved. Rumours were rife below-stairs at Frome. If the famous diamond was missing, Lord Denville, ecstatic over the coming heir, must not know about it. He and his countess had not attended a social affair since the announcement, her "being poorly,'' so Betty could not swear to the diamond's absence. But please, she begged, keep her posted.

Mathilda carefully tore the note into tiny pieces and fed them into the kitchen fire. She had not wasted her time in that guest bedchamber. Black moustache or no, the man posing as Denville was his formerly red-haired brother. And plain as the nose on her face—which even she knew to be proper plain—that great gem won by Lord Ralston at cards was the famous Denville diamond. The Honourable Bentley Frome had come to get it back, and the Master was refusing to give it up.

To her mind, that meant the brooch was up for grabs. No one would ever suspect her, and what's more, she had a pretty good notion where his lordship would keep such a valuable trophy. There would be a lock to be picked, but her Norton knew a thing or two about milling kens. There were times when a husband who knew his way about came in mighty handy...and he had recently been released from gaol.

AT DINNER THAT EVENING, Violet studied Lord Ralston's faultless apparel. She was not well-acquainted with the raiment of gentlemen, but there seemed to be no odd bulges in his smooth-fitting waistcoat that might be a diamond brooch. Could he have left it in the garment he had worn that day? In any case, if he hadn't the diamond with him, it must be in his room.

When Lady Hippolyta rose and collected the ladies, Violet slipped away instead of joining the company in the drawing-room. Now, while Lord Ralston entertained the gentlemen at their port, would be the time for a quick search of his chamber.

It was dark upstairs in Ralston's bedroom. Very dark. Her nerves on edge, Violet had that eerie feeling one gets that one is not alone. Was that the sound of a quick breath? Nonsense, she reproved herself. Only her imagination. But in any case, she would not be able to tell one waistcoat from another in the wardrobe without a candle. Feeling about on the dressing-table, she found a candlestick and the tinder-box and struck a light. She had turned towards the wardrobe when, behind her, she heard a gentle cough.

Startled, she gave a tiny scream and whirled about. In the wavering light of the candle, she saw a man sitting on the edge of Ralston's bed, twirling a black moustache. Denville!

"Odd," he remarked in a conversational tone, "how often great minds move in the same channel."

Violet collected her scattered wits and set the candle on the table. Montrose had told her how his father had acquired the diamond, and she knew at once that Denville had come on the same errand as herself.

"You've come to steal Lord Ralston's brooch!" she accused.

He shook his head. "Lady Denville's, not Ralston's. But I cannot conceive why you are doing the same. And while we are on the subject, I cannot fathom why you are pretending to be Lady Clarissa."

Violet's stomach plummeted. He knew all! Well, not all. But if she explained about Clarissa and her elopement with Edward, perhaps he would not expose her. It was worth a try, for he seemed a decent sort. He listened, rubbing his chin thoughtfully.

"Pray do not give me away," she finished. "I must remain here as Clarissa until she is safely beyond pursuit."

He nodded slowly. "Yes, I admire your loyalty to your cousin. But why are you attempting to purloin Letty—Lady Denville's diamond?"

There was nothing for it but to tell him of Montrose's problem. "If he can but hold that diamond hostage, he will force his father to make Lady Hippolyta release his inheritance. Without it, his only recourse is to marry to please his great-aunt, and he has no wish to wed Clarissa. He—he has another in mind."

"You." The moustached man shook his head. "I am afraid I cannot further that cause. My need is greater. I have given my word to Letty that I will return the brooch to her."

"But you are rich enough to buy her another! And it is her own fault she lost it. Your silly wife should not have been gaming in the first place."

Before he could reply, footsteps sounded outside in the hall and halted by the door. There was no way to escape. Bentley snuffed the candle, yanked open the mahogany wardrobe and shoved Violet inside. He squashed in with her, sadly crushing Ralston's elegant coats.

His arms were about her, holding her close as he pulled the door shut. Violet was suddenly so conscious of the man whose body pressed against hers that she shivered.

"Cold?" He breathed the word into her ear and his warm breath stirred a tendril of hair, tickling her cheek. "It must be Ralston," he whispered. "If he is preparing for bed, we are in for a long stay in his closet."

"Not if he decides to hang up his coat!" She shivered again and his arm tightened about her waist, not demanding, not teasing, but gentle and comforting. She sighed softly and rested her head against his chest. His heart was beating beneath her cheek—and she abruptly remembered she was in the arms of another woman's husband.

How could it feel so right when all was wrong? This man had a wife—a wife who was about to bear his child! She started to pull away and his arm tightened again, holding her still.

"Shh. Don't move."

Move? All at once she couldn't move, aware as she was of tiny noises in the room beyond. Scrapes, rattles, the sound of drawers sliding shut. What would they do if—or when!—Ralston opened his wardrobe and discovered them?

Bentley felt her shudder. She raised her head and her forehead brushed his chin. He touched a soothing kiss to the tip of her nose. Then, before he realized what he was about, his lips moved down to hers in the first true lover's embrace he had ever known.

Violet froze, startled, and he drew back. Good God, had he lost his wits? Playing the married man and kissing an innocent miss! What violence such an action must do to her maidenly sensibilities! He was behaving less the gentleman than Hildebrand at his most rakish. This would never do. He must be more circumspect in his dealings with Miss Violet Langford, until the day when he could confess all and beg her forgiveness.

He released his hold and Violet awoke, as though from a trance, and tore herself free. Heedlessly pushing open the wardrobe door, she flew from the closet.

The man outside in the room gave a choking cry, dropped his candle, and fell to the floor in a dead faint.

CHAPTER SIX

THE CANDLE FLARED, its flame catching the fibres of the carpet, and the resulting fire lit the features of the unconscious man.

"Montrose!" Violet exclaimed. "That nodcock! I might have known he'd try something idiotish!"

She caught up the water pitcher on Ralston's commode and threw it, not on the fire, but over Montrose's head.

Bentley hastily secured his slipping moustache, an article not designed for kissing girls in snug wardrobes, and stamped out the small blaze.

Montrose sat up, groggy, and picked vaguely at his soaked neckcloth.

"I thought I told you to leave this to me," Violet scolded. "I knew you'd make mice-feet of the business if you tried."

He blinked up at her. "Where am I?"

"Now why," Bentley mused, "did I expect to hear those exact words?" He raised Hildebrand's quizzing glass to inspect Montrose, took one look at the distorted image and dropped the glass to the end of his grosgrain ribbon. However, the effect of his gesture was quelling enough.

Montrose shrank away from him. "What's he doing here?"

"I am merely another who 'Forth from his dark and lonely hiding place...cries out, Where is it?'" Bentley answered. He glanced at Violet, who flushed scarlet. "Only not so lonely."

Montrose's pale features blanched even more. "He's after it, too?"

"I fear so." Violet sat down on the side of the bed, realized what she was doing and rose quickly. "He feels he has a claim on our diamond, simply because it once belonged to his family."

"Once?" Bentley complained. "It still does."

Montrose summoned as much dignity as he could while sitting on the floor in a puddle of water. "It belongs to my father! He won it!"

This Bentley could not allow. He shook his head. "By treacherous means. I am sorry to say your father is not an honest man."

Montrose wasted no time in denial. "What's your interest in my father's diamond? You have all the blunt you need!"

"Do not tell me you don't know where he got it."

"He won it fair and square. At piquet."

Bentley favoured him with a sad smile and shook his head. "I fear not." He perched on the edge of the dressing-table and swung a negligent leg. "Your father may have played fairly, though I doubt it, but Lady Denville did not wager that brooch. It was merely pledged, to be redeemed in a week when she received her quarterly allowance and could pay off her vowels.''

''I don't believe you.''

''Nor do I!'' Violet suddenly sided with Montrose. ''A man in Lord Ralston's position—a peer—would not lie!''

Bentley bowed slightly without rising. ''If that is your belief. I only state my case. The brooch belongs to Lady Denville.''

''But—but I *need* that diamond!'' Montrose cried.

Violet turned to him, shrugging. ''The rig is up, Monty,'' she said. ''Lord Denville knows all.''

''All?'' Montrose stared at her, shaken. ''He knows you are not Clarissa?''

''If I did not before,'' Bentley told him kindly, ''I would now.'' He turned to Violet. ''Surely you see it would be folly to ally yourself to such a gapwit.''

Montrose stared at him, the epithet passing over his head. ''You know?'' he repeated.

''Aye. 'Let down the curtain: the farce is done.' Sorry,'' Bentley remarked to Violet apologetically. ''I couldn't resist.''

She helped Montrose to his feet. ''Oh, do be quiet, my lord. What are we to do now?''

He looked down at the charred rug. In stamping out the fire, he had also stamped on the candle, crushing melted wax into Ralston's carpet, which was now soaked with the water Monty was wringing from his neckcloth. ''May I suggest we remove this conclave to the hall? Ralston may return at any moment and I do not feel he will be pleased.''

Violet pushed Montrose towards the door. "Yes, let us leave. I'd rather not be part of the next scene."

Bentley snuffed the candle she had left burning on the dressing-table and followed them out into the dark hall. "'So part we sadly in this troublous world.'" He waited expectantly and she did not fail.

"'To meet with joy in sweet Jerusalem?' I had rather hoped it would be sooner."

He chuckled and tried to slip his arm about her shoulder to give her a quick squeeze, but she jerked away.

"Much as I hate 'to leave this keen encounter of our wits,'" she said, "I think we'd best disperse and quickly. I hear voices on the stairs. Come along, Montrose, let's not dawdle."

Bentley watched them pass beneath the sconce down the hall, the candlelight making a halo of her soft brown curls. He drew a deep breath and paraphrased a line from a poem he'd recently read. 'Oh, how sweet it is to find The one just suited to our mind.' If only this masquerade were done!

THE NEXT MORNING, Violet breakfasted on toast and tea in her bedchamber. She admitted to herself frankly that she could not face Lord Denville again until she could bring to order her chaotic feelings. She was conscious of some very upsetting emotions regarding the notorious earl.

Unexpected shoals lay ahead if she continued to explore the heady pleasures of the mating of their minds. Never before had she known that sense of oneness, of understanding, as though she and he existed in a world apart from all others, sharing thoughts both comfortable and familiar. She felt the quicksand beneath her feet and drew back like a salted snail. Too late. Violet was nothing if not truthful, even with herself, and she sighed as she accepted the fact that she was far from indifferent to the charms of an infamous rake. But never would she be content as the mistress of a married man, even were she willing to cast her reputation to the wind, which she definitely was not!

Well, she was no silly pea-goose. Denville would never know of her stupid infatuation, nor would anyone else.

After discovering there were men like Denville and Bentley Frome, how dismal to think of marrying Montrose. And if she did not? The years stretched before her, empty years of spinsterhood eking out her living as a companion to Clarissa, and then as governess to Clarissa's children. Never to have a family of her own... It was a melancholy thought, but not devastating unless she permitted it to become so. And she would not. She'd forget— No, not forget. She'd store Denville in her memories along with his red-haired brother, her knight errant, and lock them away until she could include them in day-dreams without so much pain.

Meanwhile she rose briskly, brushing the last of her toast crumbs from her lap onto the tray. The sun was shining, and by now the other guests at Branleigh would be off to the race meets. What she needed was a walk in the fresh air while she tried to come up with a new scheme to get the brooch. Somehow, she shrank from another visit to Lord Ralston's bedchamber.

She went down the curving front staircase and had let herself out through one of the French windows in the drawing-room before she saw someone else pacing along the terrace. Even without her spectacles, she knew from the set of his shoulders that it was Denville. She should go back in at once . . . but her feet refused to move.

The man reached the end of the terrace and turned—and she could have sworn that above his black moustache he wore a pair of eyeglasses. He saw her, and the spectacles, if he had them, vanished into a pocket as he hastened towards her. He raised his quizzing glass instead, but dropped it at once.

"For a moment there," he said by way of greeting, "you looked so like the fair Titania in the morning sunlight that I was sure you were she."

Violet felt a rising blush reach her cheeks. "My lord, you must not address me so."

He looked around. "Not here on the terrace at any rate, in plain view of that housemaid whom I see peering from an upper window. Come, let us wander off 'Beneath the milk-white thorn that scents the evening gale.' Well, to the morning rose garden, anyway, where we may 'muse on nature with a poet's eye.'"

She hesitated, half turning back to the house. His manner was far too warm. It was madness to converse at all with Denville, even madder to linger with him in the garden. Why did she not just run away?

"This is insanity, my lord."

"I know. But this sunshine is too fair to waste. Pray come with me. 'I know a bank Whereon the wild thyme blows, Where oxlips and the nodding violet grows.'"

"'Quite over-canopied with luscious woodbine...'" Despite her better judgement, she nearly finished the quote. "No, really, my lord. I must not walk in the gardens with you."

"I could try another poem. 'Shall I compare thee to a summer's day? Thou art more lovely and more temperate.'"

"I shan't remain temperate if you continue in this vein!" She realized that somehow they had stepped from the terrace down to one of the paths in the shrubbery by the side of the house. She stopped short. "My lord Denville, you forget. I—I am betrothed to Montrose. And I cannot dally among rose-bushes with a married man!"

He took her arm and guided her firmly along. "I need to speak to you most seriously about this betrothal. Surely you can see this alliance with young Montrose will not do."

Although she had begun to come to the same conclusion herself, it remained her one defence. For a moment, she tried frantically to find an excuse for her engagement. "He may not appear to you to be the answer to a maiden's dream, but—but 'Love looks not with the eyes, but with the mind.'"

"How can a female of your intelligence even think of marrying such a one?" He sounded quite disgusted. "'He has not so much brain as earwax.'"

Violet choked on a giggle and abruptly became sober. It was time and more to put an end to this perilous conversation. "I must marry someone," she said, pulling away the arm he had drawn through his. "Marriage is the only recourse for a lady of quality. You are married yourself. How—how is Lady Letitia? I daresay you are looking forward to becoming a father!"

"Demme, I forgot about that!" exclaimed the startled gentleman. "I must admit, the prospect of becoming a father is the furthest thing from my mind."

Violet stared at him, blank with shock. Forget his wife? The woman who carried his child? How low could a philandering libertine sink! She turned and fled from him into the safety of the house.

Bentley gazed after her. He was tempted to call her back and reveal his identity, but he was suddenly unsure of her reaction. She was betrothed to Ralston's son. She was on Montrose's side; she had made that clear the night before. It would be quite in the cards for her to unveil him to her fiancé, if not to Ralston. A pretty botch that would make of it. And he *had* to get back Letitia's paste stone.

"'Lord,'" he muttered. "'What fools these mortals be.'"

As Bentley wandered off along the terrace, a stealthy figure slid out from behind a corner of the shrubbery, brushing twigs and dead leaves out of his hair with an impatient hand. Seemed like hours he'd spent, waiting for that moustached dandy and his classy mort to go away. And what were they doing here, anyhow? Mathilda said they'd all be off to the races. He hesitated, settling his frayed nerves, for they'd near as naught caught him. He remembered seeing Mathilda at an upper window and his annoyance cooled. She must have been trying to warn him.

But should he go ahead with this devilish task she'd set him? He looked back up at the window. There she was, waving him on, giving him his orders. He knew better than to disobey. He ducked down, crouched nearly double, and began to creep along the path between the hedges until he reached a point just below Lord Ralston's ground-floor study.

The window sash stood ajar. Mathilda had done her job. He raised up cautiously and peered within. The room was empty. Finding an easy toehold in the rough stone of the wall, he got a good grip on the windowsill and hoisted himself up. Another minute, a barked shin and some scraped knuckles later, and he was inside.

The room was exactly as she had described it: heavy drapes, a massive mahogany desk and chair, carved wainscotting all around the room. Once more he marvelled at his luck in getting leg-shackled to such a needle-witted wench. Thanks to her, he was about to retire in comfort for the rest of his life.

Now to find that safe box. He knew where to look, for Mathilda had located the rather obvious secret panel behind which it lay hidden some days ago while cleaning the room. Only the fact that she had as yet failed to find the key to its heavy padlock had kept her from getting into Lord Ralston's cache.

Norton wasn't sure he could pick the lock, but he was about to give it the devil of a try. The barkeep down at the tavern in the village had lent him a kit of bent bits of metal and given him a few lessons in exchange for the promise of a cut. If those tricky tools wouldn't open it, he'd carry the whole box off. That's what he'd wanted to do in the first place, but Mathilda said no. Leave it be, right where it is, she'd said. Don't take no chances being caught with that there box. Open the lock, take out the flash brooch that's inside, lock the box up and away again. Then get out before no one's the wiser.

He was kneeling before the panel, looking for the knob in the carving that sprang the mechanism, when heavy footsteps stopped at the door. In the flicker of an eyelid, he was under Ralston's mammoth desk.

LADY HIPPOLYTA STOMPED UP to the door of her blasted nephew's study, wheezing gently, for she was not built for prolonged activity of any kind. She made no effort to be quiet. After all, who would question her actions in her own house? Besides, she knew Ralston had gone off to the races with his guests. Only Lady Clarissa and Lord Denville had remained behind. At first she had suspected an indiscreet assignation, but Clarissa had come in and gone up to her room. Denville, on whom she had been keeping a sharp eye, had settled in the library with a book. The coast was clear.

It was high time, she decided, to cut Ralston down to size. Since he'd won that confounded diamond he'd become positively uppity. She had thought first to annoy him by releasing Montrose's share of the estate, the only thing she, as executrix, had the power to do. On second thought, she hadn't dared to take such a chunk from the principal while the boy lacked maturity. He'd surely waste it, and the interest from the total amount of the funds barely kept Branleigh going as it was. The only solution was to separate Ralston from the dratted brooch before he sold it back to Denville. Once he gained financial freedom he'd begin to lord it over her.

To her mind, it would be a simple matter. There was just one place to keep such a valuable piece, the safe box behind the secret panel in the study. From his smug appearance lately, she deduced that Ralston believed it to be secure. He had forgot that his aunt was the widow of the former owner of that study. She knew of the panel, and she had a key to the box. Thankfully, she'd had the forethought to remove it from her late lord's key-ring immediately upon his demise.

She opened the study door and waddled in. The third panel on the right-hand wall it was, and down near the baseboard. She grunted and groaned, lowering her bulk to the floor.

NORTON WATCHED from his haven beneath the desk, his eyes wide with horror. When she twisted the proper knob, he heard the panel squeak as it moved to one side. She drew out a metal box and fitted a key into the lock while he smothered a rising howl of despair.

By pressing his head against one of the heavy carved legs of the desk, he had a clear view of what happened next. She tipped back the lid of the box and began to empty papers out onto her voluminous lap, slowly at first, then with a desperate urgency. She scrabbled about inside the box, finally turning it upside down and shaking it.

Nothing more fell out. Norton found he'd been holding his breath near to bursting his lungs, and he expelled it in a sudden whoosh. Luckily, the overstuffed lady didn't hear. She was speaking aloud, making a remark about Lord Ralston that contained words no lady should have known.

Norton looked on as she replaced the papers, relocked the box and returned it to the cubby-hole behind the wainscotting, sliding the panel back into place. With much heaving and gasping, she managed to haul herself upright, using the leg of the desk inches from Norton's nose. Pallid with fear, he cowered against the farthest corner, but her efforts were so strenuous that she failed to detect him.

Like an overloaded frigate pulling away from a dock, she pushed off from the desk. The backwash of her billowing skirts flicked his perspiring face as she wallowed towards the door. She left the room, still muttering maledictions on Ralston.

As soon as his trembling legs would hold him up, Norton crawled out from his hiding-place. Wet with the sweat of complete terror, he clambered back out the window and dropped into the shrubbery. Sneaking around to the back of the house, he bolted into the potting shed in the kitchen garden, where Mathilda had arranged to meet him.

The wife of his bosom eyed him morosely when he finished his tale.

"Not there, eh?" she asked quietly, picking up an empty flowerpot and smashing it on the floor. "And that lumping besom is after the brooch, too. Nothing else she could be looking for, not shaking that box upside down like she done."

She apostrophized briefly on the character of Lady Hippo, for that sobriquet had also occurred long ago to one of the more irreverent minions in the servants' hall and had been taken up with delight.

Mathilda Norton was not a namby-pamby wench to be defeated by a minor set-back. She sank onto one of the lower potting shelves, her chin in her hand, her devious mind at work. Absently she took up a corner of her apron and chewed on it. Norton, recognizing the signs, waited respectfully near the door. Too near. A hoe, precariously balanced against the jamb, fell with a clatter.

Clumsy. Mathilda's glance at him was sour. Always, his clumsiness interfered just when they found a comfortable situation. Only think of Frome! If Norton had to steal, why could he not have taken something worthwhile and escaped with it? Why not the Denville diamond, when it lay almost within his grasp? They could have been set up for life, instead of her worked to the bone as a housemaid and himself spending his best years in the sponging house.

Frome. An idea began to form on the edge of her mind. The Honourable Bentley had just come from Frome—without his faithful valet. Below-stairs, it was thought very odd that a man of Denville's rank would venture forth without his man. Remembering the strict and elderly Beecham, who'd held that position for over twenty years, first with Denville, then with his younger brother, Mathilda could understand why the old retainer had not been included in the present goings-on. That knaggy gadger would never for a moment condone such a chancy lark.

She sat up straight, smoothing the damp edge of her apron. A valet was needed to preserve the image of the Earl of Denville, and a valet the Honourable Bentley Frome was about to receive.

"Norton," she announced, "we're going to buy us a tavern in Lunnon East End yet."

He looked at her expectantly, hope mingled with unease on his face.

"The tale I been told is that Lord Denville's valet isn't here because he met with an accident on the way. Well, he's all recovered and he'll be here tonight, because you'll be him."

"Me? You're all about in your head!"

"Yes, you, clodpole. Didn't I just say so?"

Norton's mouth gaped in horror and Mathilda frowned at him. Her Norton might be all right on the physical side, but he was not strong in the brain.

"Why ever not?" she demanded.

"But I never was no valet! I'm a footman."

She sneered. "Yes, you are. A footman living with a pack of sots in a cheap inn. Don't argue with me. I got it all thought out. As Lord Denville's valet, you'll have the run of the place. It'll be dead easy for you to sneak into the Master's bedchamber and find where he keeps that there brooch."

Norton put his finger on the flaw in her plan. "But I won't be Lord Ralston's man. How'd I explain being in his room if I get caught?"

"Birdbrain." Mathilda's lips curled in disgust. "You got more hair than wit. You say as how you was lost and mistook the way, being new in the house and all. And that diamond won't be hidden. His lordship don't know anyone is out to steal his brooch."

He reminded her of Lady Hippo opening the safe box, and she waved a deprecating hand.

"That's family. Nothing to do with us. You can be in and out of there in a trice. Once you're inside the house, between us we'll have that diamond in no time!"

Norton hesitated. "I reckon I could apply for the job. How do you know he'll hire me?"

"Hire you!" Mathilda snorted. "You go and put on your Sunday suit that I kept for you and come back here. I'll have it all set up."

Great was Norton's faith in his crafty helpmate, and he hesitated no longer. He squared his shoulders. "I'll do it," he said.

PEEK-A-BOO!

Free Gifts For You!

*Look inside—Right Now!
We've got something
special just for you!*

(U-H-RG-07/91)

GIFTS

There's no cost— and no obligation to buy anything!

We'd like to send you free gifts to introduce you to the benefits of the Harlequin Reader Service®: free home delivery of brand-new Harlequin Regency Romance™ novels months before they're available in stores, and at a savings from the cover price!

Accepting our free gifts places you under no obligation to buy anything ever. You may cancel the Reader Service at any time, even just after receiving your free gifts, simply by writing "cancel" on your statement or returning a shipment of books to us at our cost. But if you choose not to cancel, every other month we'll send you four more Harlequin Regency Romance™ novels, and bill you just $2.64* apiece—and there's **no** extra charge for shipping and handling. There are **no** hidden extras!

IN THE GREAT LIBRARY at Branleigh, Bentley pressed the slipping moustache back into place. It seemed less secure, as if the spirit-gum adhesive was wearing out. He couldn't stay here much longer. He'd have to make another try for that black-velvet-covered jewellery case. Only it would be no use to search his lordship's room now; he had seen the square corners of the box bulging in Ralston's pocket when the man left for the races with the rest of the party.

The only time he felt sure Ralston hadn't the brooch on his person was when he wore his smooth-fitting evening togs. Tonight, while the party played at cards, he'd try again.

He grinned, recalling the events of the night before. He could still feel that warm, slim body in his arms. Strange sensations had stirred within him, there in Ralston's wardrobe. Never had he felt so Hildebrandish! Kissing Violet had seemed the most natural act in the world. He wondered, with a touch of surprise, when he had passed from a sense of delighted companionship to a far warmer desire to repeat that kiss.

He'd have to do something about her betrothal to Montrose, though he had to admire her loyalty to him. And for a delicate female like her to undertake an adventurous masquerade to help another! Such an enterprising girl was utterly wasted on a stick like Montrose.

Throwing his book down on the table, he paced the length of the bookroom, chafing under his forced disguise and his inability to declare himself here and now. Devilish difficult to woo a lady who believed you to be married! And his slip this morning, forgetting Letitia and her baby! A pretty bumble-broth he was making of the whole affair. It would not be wonderful if she never spoke to him again, even in his own character.

Restless, he wandered out of the library and roamed the empty great hall, finally going up the curving stairs to his own room. He pulled open his door and stopped, amazed to see a housemaid seated in the padded chair by the window.

It was the same woman as before, and there was something oddly familiar about her now that he saw her close at hand. He caught himself reaching for his spectacles and squinted at her instead.

"Don't I know you from somewhere?"

She smiled most unpleasantly. "Indeed you do, Master Bentley. On account of your family, my Norton got sent to the gaol."

"Norton?" Good God, now he remembered her. Mathilda, the former upper housemaid at Frome, married to the footman who'd stolen Denville's silver cow creamer. Was he to be unmasked all too soon? "Your Norton is a thief," he parried, playing for time.

Her smile did not waver. "That is quite beside the point. I hear as how you haven't brought Beecham with you. You need a valet, and I think it would be very nice if you hired on my Norton. He needs the job."

"I will do no such thing. I can't help it if your Norton is a bumbling fool!" There might be more to it than this. What did she really want for her silence?

Mathilda rose, tight-lipped. "My Norton don't pretend to be someone he ain't, my *Lord Denville*. He'll do just fine for the likes of you." She walked out of the room.

Bentley looked after her. That housemaid had him trussed up. He looked at the wrinkled and soiled neckcloths and shirts piled by his bed. Unused to packing, he had not brought enough, and he would soon be reduced to wearing a barrel if someone did not take charge of cleaning and pressing his wardrobe. He could use a valet, and what better way to keep the dangerous Nortons under his watchful eye?

One needn't, he decided, reject the only bit of luck he was likely to get.

CHAPTER SEVEN

ACROSS THE HALL from Lady Hippolyta's chambers, Violet huddled in her room. When the rest of the house party left that morning for the racetrack, she had pleaded a headache, fearing to meet some friend of Clarissa's there who might recognize her. Now she had a genuine headache, and it was all Lord Denville's fault. Discovering that a hardened rake could actually forget the wife who was bearing his child, while he sought his pleasure with another, had shaken her badly.

She was concerned—no, frightened!—by the fatal attraction she felt for Lord Denville. Oh, why could it not be his brother, Bentley, who visited Branleigh instead of the married Hildebrand? Never had she met a man who could cast such a spell. Like the character in Sheridan's *Duenna*, she 'was struck all of a heap.' She went further, quoting Jonathan Swift, 'Lord! I wonder what fool it was that first invented kissing.'

Violet caught herself abruptly. Now she was quoting when she was alone! Would she ever again be able to read a poem or see a play without sensing Denville's magnetic presence? If it had been the red-haired Bentley who held her in his arms, she would have welcomed his advances. The realization frightened her even more, for she barely knew the Honourable Bentley Frome, and he must have forgot her completely by now. As she must forget both Fromes! Far better to marry Montrose than to live in constant fear of her virtue!

It wouldn't be so terrible; Monty was a weakling, but she'd manage to be happy as his wife, once she never had to meet Denville again. She and Monty had always been friends, and she imagined they could rub along tolerably well together. What he lacked in forceful character he made up for in other less exciting ways. And she'd be safe at Branleigh. Branleigh. What she had seen of the house had impressed her immensely. Only think, she coaxed herself, to be mistress of this wondrous place one day! Was Montrose too great a price to pay? She'd be a fool to let him go. A fool!

The luncheon gong chimed through the halls, saving her further self-chastisement, but bringing a more current problem. She would have to see Denville—and face Clarissa's godmother. Her mirror reflected such a pale countenance and shadowed eyes that she dreaded Lady Hippolyta's probing gaze. She smoothed her hair and patted rice powder over the dark circles, but only looked worse. Biting her lips and pinching her cheeks restored a bit of her colour.

The meal was every bit as daunting as she had feared. Only the three of them were present. Lady Hippolyta loomed at the foot of the table, massive in puce *velours natté* with a blond lace tucker. Like a majestic hippopotamus... With difficulty, Violet squelched that thought. Hippopotamuses did not wear Parisian mob-caps of fine linen, with puffed crowns and ruffled borders. Plain ones, perhaps... She stifled an hysterical giggle.

Her hostess's penetrating gaze shifted to her from Denville, who was nervously twirling that silly moustache, and Violet lost all tendency to mirth. Lady Hippolyta stared at her for a moment and then turned back to Denville with an eye that could have pried open the oysters in the broth they were consuming.

"How's your head?" she demanded. Her pointed gaze moved yet again to Violet, who felt her colour rise. "I trust," her ladyship continued, speaking to Denville, "you've sense enough not to risk having it cracked open again."

He choked over his soup and had some difficulty with his moustache. Violet knew her cheeks were blazing as she recalled how Lady Hippo—oh, dear, Lady Hippolyta—thought he'd acquired that headache.

Her ladyship, satisfied that she had thoroughly discomfited them both, sat back and slurped her soup.

Denville made a gallant recovery and used his napkin to pat the broth from his moustache. "You may be assured of that, my lady. Lightning never strikes twice in the same place." He tried to catch Violet's eye.

Lady Hippolyta plied her spoon, hunting an elusive oyster before answering. "Certainly it does," she said. "It has found that tallest elm on the east drive twice in the last ten years. Let that be a lesson to you. You're more vulnerable than a tree."

Violet thought she heard him make a small appreciative noise, but kept her eyes on her plate, refusing to look up. She would not fall again into his trap. Even without her spectacles, she could see him clearly enough across the table, and if he smiled at her...

He tried a different tack. "I saw Montrose as he left this morning. Quite a Tulip of the Ton, is he not?"

Lady Hippolyta humphed. "He doesn't look like any flower I ever saw."

"I merely meant he was fine as fivepence."

"Can't be a fivepence," she returned. "He's not a coin, he's a man. Or thinks he is. I never saw a fivepence yet that was worth much more than a groat."

His voice remained serious. "I daresay you'd prefer him to remain here at Branleigh rather than swank about London. Ah, well, the grass is always greener in the next pasture."

She snorted. "No, it's not. Grass is always the same colour in adjoining fields."

He was deliberately baiting the old lady! In spite of herself, Violet glanced up and met impish devils of mischief dancing in his eyes. She looked away quickly. How could he! Then she realized that Lady Hippolyta was enjoying herself and so was Denville. He couldn't resist plying his fatal charm on any female who would listen to him! Well, she was on to him now.

"I understand you are an outdoorsman," her ladyship was saying, sounding actually cordial. "We have some fine fishing in our trout stream. Feel free to try your hand.''

''I will,'' he replied. ''My favourite sport. May I proffer a thousand thanks?''

''Go right ahead,'' she said. ''But I haven't the time to sit here and listen to them.'' She hoisted herself from her chair.

Violet rose precipitately, having no desire to be left alone with Denville. She hurried into the hall after Lady Hippolyta who had begun to climb the stairs.

''Always had a soft spot for a rake,'' her ladyship wheezed, pulling herself up by the banister. ''Mind you, that's no advice for you, miss. You steer clear of him.''

''I intend to,'' Violet assured her. And at the time, she meant it.

BENTLEY FOLLOWED them out of the room, feeling inordinately cheerful. He had acquitted himself well on the battlefield, he thought, quite as well as even Hildebrand might have done.

He had not made much progress in recovering Letitia's confounded brooch. He paused at the foot of the stairs, then began to mount slowly. Oh, the devil. He was letting himself become sadly distracted by Miss Violet Langford. It was time he got back to the business that brought him to Branleigh. Had he really detected the bulge of the black-velvet case in Ralston's pocket that morning or had he merely leaped at an excuse to tarry here for the pleasure of playing ''top the quote'' with that delightful miss? Any number of things could create just such a bulge. He was wasting a beautiful opportunity to explore his lordship's room in broad daylight. He stepped up his pace.

VIOLET, trailing behind the slow-moving Lady Hippolyta, tried hard to keep up her resentment against Lord Denville. Indeed, he shouldn't be trying to steal back his wife's diamond. Montrose said Lord Ralston had won it legitimately and she believed him. Denville should *pay* his wife's debt. She felt more upset by his dishonourable actions than she should have been. After all, he was a degenerate rake and dangerously attractive. She resolved to avoid him completely until she was safely wed to Montrose.

They reached the second landing and Lady Hippolyta continued along the hall. When she reached her own room, she waited to see Violet go into hers. *Doesn't trust me,* Violet thought, *or rather, she doesn't trust Denville.* She gave Lady Hippo a brilliant, though artificial, smile and went in. Lady Hippolyta's heavy footsteps moved on and Violet, curious, opened her door a crack and peeked out.

Her ladyship was entering her nephew's chamber, not her own. Now why... Violet knew a sudden flash of intuition. Lady Hippo was after the Denville diamond, too!

Montrose claimed his father's manner had become unbearable since he'd acquired the fabulous stone. His lordship even contradicted his formidable aunt. Of course, she would want him parted from it.... Violet's fists clenched. Lady Hippo had no right to deprive poor Montrose of his chance to come into his fortune for such a paltry reason. Her ladyship must not find that waistcoat pocket!

Then, slowly, Violet's fists unclenched. She had seen Lord Ralston leave for the races that morning and had glimpsed the distinctive pattern of that particular garment beneath his coat. Lady Hippolyta was wasting her time—and Violet had better not waste her own. Tonight, when Ralston sat at cards wearing his evening togs, she would make another try for his waistcoat.

She remained at her door, bound by a sense of urgency. So much depended on Lady Hippolyta's appearance when she left that room. A look of triumph would mean a defeat for Montrose—at least temporarily; one of annoyance would signal a victory. Violet couldn't imagine Lady Hippo looking discouraged.

Minutes crept by, and then stealthy footsteps approached from the landing. She peeked out. Denville! And he was heading directly for the lion's den. Only think what would happen when he opened Ralston's door and faced Lady Hippolyta!

She couldn't leave him to his doom. She rushed out and grabbed him by the arm. "Lady Hippo is in there!"

He looked down at her, twirling his moustache in a startled way.

"Good God. I must thank you!"

"Never mind that now." She pulled him towards her door. "She may come out! She must not see us together!"

"No, indeed." He seemed much struck. "By all means, let us hide. I trust you have a wardrobe?"

He followed her into her room, and she closed the door firmly. "There'll be no nonsense. Stay away from me."

He obliged, remaining by the door. "Charming spot," he remarked, looking about as he adjusted his neckcloth and smoothed the wrinkles she had made in his coat sleeve. "They have done you well. Far better than the digs they provided for me."

"I am a welcome guest. Do, please, keep your voice down."

He obliged. "Aye, the dragon lies in wait behind me, ever watching. She'd be in ault should she catch me in here. She is one 'Whose horrid image doth unfix my hair And make my seated heart knock at my ribs.'"

Violet felt a twinge of resentment. "No such thing. I believe you enjoy jousting with her. She only wishes to preserve my character. I've rather come to like her."

"As have I, but not as a steady diet. Avoid her, my dear, lest you are singed. She is a fire-breather."

"That she is not. Merely protective, which I needn't remind you is not out of line."

"Meaning I am? But to return to Lady Hippo, 'Tis distance lends enchantment.'"

Violet paused, arrested. "Now who said that?"

He grinned. "Caught you. Thomas Campbell, no doubt a near-sighted gentleman."

She giggled and smiled up at him before she could stop. A mistake.

He pretended to stagger dramatically. "Don't do that without warning! You should be careful how you smile at a fellow so recently scorned. He might feel compelled to kiss you on the spot!"

Somewhat rattled, Violet stepped back. This was not going at all well. Why, oh why, did all her resolution flee when she found herself alone with this dangerous man? Oh, the sooner she married Montrose the better for all concerned! Had she no willpower at all? The man seemed bent on ruining her! "My lord," she said, her lips tight, "I fear you forget you are a married man."

He touched his black moustache. "There, my lady, you have put your finger on the crux of the matter. But may I hasten to assure you, paraphrasing the great Shakespeare, I am a gentleman on whom you may build an absolute trust."

She didn't believe him for a moment, but her curiosity got the better of her. "Where is that? Tell me, that I may argue the point."

"*Macbeth.*"

"Ah. Then 'yet do I fear thy nature.'"

He beamed down on her. "Oh, I must change plays! 'O wonderful, wonderful, and most wonderful wonderful! and yet again wonderful, and after that, out of all whooping!'"

Before she knew what he was about, she was swept into his arms and kissed soundly on the cheek. He released her at once, but the damage was done. Her heart pounded like a wild thing trying to escape its stays, and she gasped for air.

Truly, the man was impossible! No wonder he had garnered such an infamous reputation. And why, she wondered, had she stupidly let it happen? Even this friendly salutation, such as one might give to a sister...

Then, before she could protest, he corrected that deficiency. Once more he drew her to him, this time with slow, relentless purpose.

His arms were warm and strong, his breath soft upon her cheek. Something she had never known before soared within her as his firm lips met hers. This was no casual kiss in a wardrobe. This, she knew, was real.

"You're too damned lovely," he whispered. "'A violet by a mossy stone... Fair as a star, when only one Is shining in the sky.'"

Violet tried to push him away, grasping at the comparative safety of their game. "'Violets plucked, the sweetest rain Makes not fresh nor grow again.'"

"'A hit, a very palpable hit.'" She felt him stiffen. His moustache had tickled her nose and she sneezed, utterly shattering the spell.

"Oh, the devil!" he exclaimed. "How glad I'll be once I'm rid of the confounded thing!"

Violet took advantage of the broken mood and pulled away, her thoughts not on moustaches. "My lord, you—you should not have done that."

"Indeed not." He twirled the end of the moustache and straightened his neckcloth, but he sounded as shaken as she felt. "It seemed a good idea at the time. I pray you'll accept my humblest apologies."

She drew herself up and addressed him severely. "I know that gentlemen may flirt with married ladies with impunity, but it is quite beyond anything to kiss defenceless young females in their bedchambers!"

"Or in wardrobes?" he suggested incorrigibly.

She flushed. "It was not my fault that we were so thrown together."

"You are the one hiding me in your chamber," he countered. He shook his head. "Not at all the thing, even when masquerading as one's cousin."

She turned away, answering with some difficulty. "You must know this masquerade is not of my choosing. I despise deceit in any form and hope I may never meet with it again."

He was suddenly so silent that she looked back at him. He seemed to be making up his mind to speak, but the sounds of returning carriages crunching on the drive below her window stopped his words. From the hall came the creak and slam of a door, then the clump of Lady Hippolyta's footsteps going past.

Violet clutched his arm. "Wait," she whispered. "Do not go until she is safely away."

"Indeed," he assured her *sotto voce,* "I have no desire to go at all." But some of the gaiety was gone from his voice.

ALL GAIETY had gone from Violet. This entire affair had gone too far, and she meant to put an end to it at once. Montrose had returned with the others and now, before she lost her resolve, she had to speak to him.

She found him wandering aimlessly along the terrace, and informed him that she was willing to marry him at once.

Montrose gaped at her. "Right now? Here?"

"Not at this moment." She fought back a desire to box his ears, a desire she feared might grow with the years. "As soon as you can locate a parson."

Fervently he seized her hands. "Violet! Do you mean that? You'll marry me now while my father thinks you are Clarissa?"

"Monty, we must tell him the truth. I will tell him as soon as we are wed."

He paled. "You would not!"

"Of course I will. This is not a masquerade that can be kept up forever."

"Only until I have that diamond in my hands. Promise me that," he begged. "We must keep our secret until then."

It seemed to Violet that he was more concerned with the diamond than with marrying her. But, she reminded herself, he had offered for her before Lord Ralston had suggested his wedding gift. And if she was going to marry Montrose anyway, what difference did it make? What difference did anything make? She left Montrose on the terrace and ran up to her room, where she could let loose the tears that threatened to overwhelm her.

Montrose took out his watch with fingers that shook so badly that he nearly dropped it. Ages until dinner. He had plenty of time to run into the village and find the parson. He set off at top speed.

Two weary hours later, he dragged his tired feet into the village tavern. The local parson had been out making calls on his parishioners, and Montrose had trailed him, missing the elderly man of the cloth at every stop. Now he had also missed his dinner, and he was famished enough to settle for boiled mutton. At the moment, he wished all churchmen to the devil, particularly this one, who showed no signs of coming to rest.

As he sank onto a bench by the long trestle-table in the centre of the room, his eye fell on a man dressed in sober black who sat near the bar quaffing ale. A thoroughly respectable-looking man, he might have been a footman in his Sunday best...or even a preacher.

A fantastic idea lifted Montrose from his seat. Holding on to the edge of the table, he made his way to the man's side.

"I beg your pardon, sir," he began. "Would you by any chance be a parson?"

The man drew back, his face flushing. "I would not!"

Montrose let out a long breath. "In that case," he asked, "how would you like to earn a quick five pounds?"

BENTLEY LEFT HIS ROOM at the dinner hour, resplendent in black coat, satin knee-breeches and striped hose. He felt rather smug, for he had ruined only one of his last three neckcloths while achieving an effect that was at least not too different from Hildebrand's country style. He had one neckcloth left. The feckless Norton might yet prove useful, not that a perfidious ex-footman could be expected to do a proper job on neckcloths. It was a strong incentive to settle this brooch business as soon as possible.

At the head of the grand staircase he met Lord Ralston, and slipped into his character of Hildebrand, Earl of Denville and husband of Lady Letitia. This last he considered vital, to convince Ralston that his threat to expose her to a furious spouse held no water. He pressed the moustache securely into place and gave the drooping side a twirl. This action seemed to annoy Ralston, who planted his feet challengingly.

Bentley put on his most affable expression. "Good evening, my lord." It did not go over with any great success.

"Have you made up your mind to make me a fair offer for that brooch?" Ralston demanded.

Bentley raised his eyebrows as well as Hildebrand's quizzing glass. It would never do to allow Ralston to suspect he had plans other than to redeem the brooch with good British blunt. "I may be prepared to pay

Let—my wife's debt to you," he replied, equivocating cautiously. "I expect you then to return her brooch as was arranged at the time of her loss."

Ralston sneered. "Pish! All London knows by now that I won that brooch fair and square. I've seen to that, and I mean to have its full value. Give me your answer by the end of the week, Denville, or I shall sell it elsewhere."

He strode down the stairs. Bentley watched him go. *It's midsummer moon with you, Ralston,* he thought. *Tonight I won't fail. That I promise.*

In the dining hall, Bentley found himself once more seated by Lady Beatrix Redgrave. He glanced at the far end of the table and fancied he detected a self-satisfied smirk on Lady Hippolyta's face. Drat, he wished he could put on his spectacles so he could see for sure. It would be just like the old harridan to throw him to the wolves to keep him from her supposed god-daughter.

He looked across the table at Violet, who studiously avoided catching his eye. With a sense of pleasure, he noted that she wore a demure sprig muslin round gown trimmed with blush-pink satin roses, and that her soft brown hair had been freshly curled. Dainty as a spring flower, compared to the be-rouged and bedizened Lady Redgrave beside him, with her loose chestnut curls and looser morals.

But why did Violet look so pale? He longed to put on his spectacles. Almost, she appeared to have been weeping. Surely not because he had kissed her. Had someone seen him leave her room? Lady Hippolyta?

No, she'd have spoken to him. Or would she? Lord, in what an excessively awkward position his importunities had placed her. Never had the evils of his situation come home to him more forcibly.

Beatrix Redgrave, not one to be ignored, addressed him, thin-lipped. "We missed your presence at the race meet today."

He dragged his eyes from Violet's face. "I fear a headache prevented my going."

"Headache?" She cast a venomous glance across the table. "Or a more pressing interest?"

Bentley felt a wave of fury, and barely in time recognized the pitfall before him. He regarded Lady Redgrave with raised eyebrows. His own unconsciously tightened lips had caused the moustache to slip, and he gave it a push and a negligent Hildebrand twirl.

"You cannot mean that green girl in the dowdy muslin?" He managed a laugh. "My dear Lady Redgrave, she is the betrothed of the son of our host. What can you think of me?" He remembered, too late, that the guilty 'doth protest too much,' but she didn't seem to notice.

Some of the ice melted in her gaze, but not all. "Who else, then?" Her eyes travelled along the table, coming to rest suddenly on the sultry brunette who had pressed the direction to her room into his hand that first evening. He shrugged slightly and sacrificed her with a mental apology. Remembering the note she had written, he decided she probably deserved it.

He twirled his moustache again. "Surely you cannot expect me to bandy about the name of a lady."

To his relief, Lady Redgrave settled back with an unpleasant smile. Almost, but not quite, he felt sorry for the brazen dark-eyed lady who now would feel the brunt of her animosity.

That he ought to be ashamed of his conduct, Bentley knew full well. The Hildebrand within him bade fair to taking over completely, a thing not to be thought of! Being Hildebrand for a time was well enough, but he was far more content to be Bentley. He now lived for the day when he could return to himself.

He stole a glance across the table. What a thoroughly delightful damsel was Miss Violet Langford. Indeed wonderful beyond whooping, one he had never believed to exist. And one, he was beginning to realize, who was the only woman for him. Life with her would be one long game of wits; Shakespeare alone would last them a lifetime! There would never be a dull moment with such a needle-witted opponent—if only he could make the transition from Denville to Bentley without the loss of her respect. Her flat statement concerning deceit rankled in his mind. His one hope was that her masquerade might cancel the onus of his own.

Driven by the fear that he had put himself beyond the pale of even her friendship, he knew an overwhelming desire to speak with her. When the ladies withdrew at last, he muttered an excuse and hurried out into the hall, hoping to catch her up before she entered the drawing-room. He was stopped by a beaming butler.

"You'll be pleased to know, my lord," Hepworth announced, "that your valet has recovered and is now here."

Bentley halted, somewhat taken aback. So Norton, ex-footman and gaolbird, had already moved in and been accepted by the Branleigh servants. He had underestimated the redoubtable Mathilda. He could not get rid of the man now without difficulty. Thanking Hepworth absently, he turned away.

Why was that housemaid so determined to get her Norton employed by him? She must know the position could hardly be permanent, two or three days at most. The man would be dismissed abruptly the moment Bentley was clear of Branleigh. Obviously, it was a ploy to get the man into the house. And Norton *was* a thief. There was only one thing in Branleigh that Bentley knew of valuable enough to attract such a man—Letitia's brooch. Mathilda and Norton were from Frome; they knew the value of the real diamond.

So, he thought, more contenders enter the ring. It would almost be worth losing to them if he could only see their faces when they tried to sell that worthless hunk of glass. But it would be fatal to Letitia if the story became known. He had to retrieve the fake stone before Norton, Mathilda, Lady Hippolyta, Ralston, or Montrose and Violet had it appraised. Appalled at the rising number of competitors, he loped back to his room, taking the stairs two at a time.

The latest entry was seated by the window, at ease in the chair once occupied by Mathilda. Bentley started to raise Hildebrand's quizzing glass, then squinted at Norton instead.

"Ah, yes," he said. "I do remember you. You are the footman who pawned a silver cow creamer belonging to the Earl of Denville in order to place a wager on a horse."

Norton had risen to his feet, conscious of the status of the Honourable Bentley Frome. He swallowed and began to bluster.

"If that there nag 'ad 'ad three good legs, I wouldn't be 'ere now." He brought up an old grievance. "And I was took off without no reference."

Bentley seated himself in the chair. "You certainly won't get one from me."

"That there seems to be my fate." Norton's brow darkened. "It's my 'ope I'll not be needing no more references after milling this 'ere ken."

"No, indeed. You'll go straight to Newgate. However, since you are here, you may lay out my morning togs."

"I don't know nothin' about your clothes. I'm a footman, not a blasted valet."

Bentley shrugged. "All right, I'll dress myself, but you can do my laundry."

"'oo, me?"

"Certainly, you. It will be thought very odd belowstairs if you do not act like a valet. That butler..."

He left the rest unsaid but Norton, who had already encountered Hepworth, shuddered.

"Gimme your dirty clothes."

Bentley loaded his arms with all the garments he had worn so far, with instructions to brush and press his coats and breeches and to launder the small mountain of neckcloths and shirts he had been piling under the bed. Norton howled.

"Get Mathilda to help you," Bentley ordered with a complete lack of sympathy. "Do you know, I'm rather glad you've come." Another thought occurred to him. He had been sleeping without the moustache. It probably would not matter if Norton saw him without it, but he had locked his door at night as a safeguard against maids bringing morning tea. He'd best continue the practice, but as he now had a valet... "Can you shave a man?" he asked hopefully.

"I shaves meself."

Bentley considered Norton's chin. "Ah, well, one can't have everything. Hop along, my good valet. I need those clothes. Don't come up in the morning until I send for you."

"Why would I want to come up 'ere?"

Bentley waggled a finger beneath the man's nose. "If I land in the bouillon owing to your failing to play your part, I shall find it necessary to report you to Mathilda. I've no doubt she has given you strict orders to act the perfect valet."

Muttering under his breath, Norton left, but once out in the hall, he proceeded with a jaunty step. There was one thing he'd do that Mathilda wouldn't know about. He had a little job for one of the nobs tomorrow night. A job worth five quid! A fortune all for himself, and all he had to do was turn his collar back to front.

CHAPTER EIGHT

BRANLEIGH AWOKE next morning to a downpour. There would be no race meet this day, and Lord Ralston's house guests milled about unhappily in the breakfast room. When Bentley entered, Ralston greeted him with a chilly eye.

"I keep nothing of value in my room, Denville."

Bentley raised puzzled brows. "I beg pardon?"

"And I'll thank you to leave all tidy next time you feel an irresistible urge to search through my belongings." Ralston moved away to the sideboard and began piling baked ham and *oeufs à la coque* on his plate without waiting for an answer.

Fortunately, for Bentley had none. He had been nowhere near Ralston's chamber. Who could have made an obvious search? Lady Hippolyta surely would be more subtle, as would Violet. It must have been done during dinner, or at least before Ralston went up, which probably eliminated the one person most likely to leave a mess—Montrose. That young man had sat at port, and then joined the ladies with the rest of the gentlemen for a thorough discussion of the races they had witnessed. Bentley couldn't see

Montrose escaping the watchful eyes of his father and aunt when there were guests to entertain.

Then a disturbing thought hit him: Mathilda and Norton. It must have been. Could they have found the brooch? No, for when he sent for Norton, the man had shown up loaded with clean neckcloths and shirts, done no doubt by his wife. From his dyspeptic expression and grudging remarks, as well as the fact that the man still remained in his service, Bentley was certain the search—if it was Norton—had been unsuccessful.

His plate filled, Bentley turned away from the sideboard and bumped straight into Lady Hippolyta. Frantic juggling prevented his coddled eggs and baked ham from cascading down her billowing superstratum, and only by burying his face in his elbow did he preserve his slipping moustache.

She watched his antics with apparent interest. "Dextrous, are you not?" she observed. "However, I fear it will do you no good. You'll require more than agility." And with this cryptic remark she trundled off, shouting to Montrose to supply her with a plate of rare beef, kippers, muffins and jam.

Bentley shuddered, and not at her appetite. She had been right behind him, close enough to hear every word Ralston had said. He watched as she manoeuvered her massive figure into the chair at the foot of the long table. Without his spectacles her broad face was a pale blur, but he could swear she fixed him with a malignant eye. There were hidden advantages to being near-sighted. Even so, he could almost feel the penetration of her gaze. No wonder Montrose and his father knuckled under to her demands.

Then, like sunshine breaking through the ominous clouds outside, Violet wandered into the room, gowned in a simple round dress of jonquil muslin sprigged with blue forget-me-nots. For once he was at a loss for an adequate quote. Shakespeare, Spenser, Milton—all failed him. He only knew he had to end his masquerade, and today.

Lady Hippolyta had better eyes than he, for she must have seen the expression on his face.

"Clarissa, my love," she called out. "Here you are at last. Come sit by me. Montrose, fill a plate for her."

Beatrix Redgrave also had excellent vision, for she attached herself to Bentley's arm and led him with a firm hand to the other end of the table. He seated himself obediently beside her, present only in body, for his thoughts centred on his new resolve and the problem of how best to reveal himself to Violet. He gave abstract answers to Lady Redgrave's chatter about the inclement weather, retaining barely enough sense to avoid her suggestions of a *tête-à-tête* in a little-used parlour she had discovered in the east wing.

VIOLET HAD BEEN close enough to see his face. With a little flutter of fear—and something else—she hurried to Lady Hippolyta's side. She picked at her breakfast, keeping her eyes lowered to her plate. Luckily, the dowager countess's form of conversation required only an audience.

"Tables are being set up in the drawing-rooms," Lady Hippolyta proclaimed to the party in general. "Penny whist will be the order of the day for those requiring entertainment. This evening we shall have a treat."

She fixed her captive audience with a commanding glare. "Lady Bingham has volunteered to play for us," she pronounced. Ignoring the uneasy shuffling of feet, she went on. "Thus we may have informal dancing. The doors between the drawing-rooms shall be opened, allowing ample space, since we have only enough for two sets of six or three of four. I am sure you will all appreciate an opportunity to practice your steps for the County Ball at Warburton Castle tomorrow evening."

The ball! In all the confusion of the past few days, Violet had forgot the County Ball, for the simple reason that she had not meant to attend. She should have slipped away home by now. Clarissa and her Edward were well on the road, perhaps even already at Gretna Green and husband and wife. But Violet knew a strong reluctance to leave and grasped thankfully at her one tie with Branleigh. Montrose needed the Denville diamond. She had to stay. She had an excuse.

And the gown! That utterly delicious confection of cloud-white sarcenet and lace over an underdress of rose-pink satin, which Simpson had folded in silver paper and placed in the trunk even though Clarissa had said Violet would not be there long enough to go to the ball.

There was even, in one of the four hatboxes, an exquisite head of pale pink gauze, with a soft plume of white ostrich feathers and satin roses that matched the trim on the gown.

Never had she attended a real ball as a genuine guest—and never had she worn such a toilette! She would feel like a fairy princess. Heat flooded her cheeks. Denville would surely flatter her with heavenly quotations...and he would stand up with her.... Without question, she would stay over at Branleigh for this one last dream to store among her memories.

"We must have waltzes this evening, Lady Bingham," Beatrix Redgrave demanded, her voice rising above the conversation at the table. "Denville, you must stand up with me."

Lady Hippolyta laid down her silver two-tined fork and addressed the shrinking Lady Bingham in stentorian tones. "You will play no waltzes! I'll have no such scandalous doings in my house. Country dances are well enough for our Regent and they are well enough for me."

Violet agreed, thankfully, but Lady Redgrave only laughed, an annoyed trill, and turned to Denville, who seemed to be attempting with little success to drink tea without dunking his moustache. "There will be waltzes at Warburton Castle, you may be certain," she said. "Indecent or no. Denville, I hold you now to perform at least two of them with me."

She patted his arm possessively, seeming unconscious of the venomous stare of the dark-haired beauty who sat across from them. Violet realized her own gaze must be equally deadly and dropped her eyes. Startled, she recognized a rush of what could only be jealousy.

For the attentions of a married man! For poor Letitia's husband! Oh, she must not! She could not want to dance those waltzes with him. His arms would be about her, his head bent towards her with that warm, teasing smile... If he solicited her hand she hadn't the least degree of certainty that she would be able to refuse.

Lady Hippolyta herded her house guests, willy-nilly, into the drawing-rooms as soon as breakfast was cleared away. The tables and cards awaited them, and her ladyship proceeded to pair off the most unlikely partners she could find. At least Violet thought so, for the Redgrave female still clung to Denville's arm. She herself had drawn Montrose, and found they faced his father and the dark-haired lady who had glared so at Beatrix Redgrave.

The lady had apparently conceded defeat and now turned her quite obvious charms on Lord Ralston. His lordship preened himself and became the bluff and hearty host.

"Ah, Lady Evans," he greeted her genially. "So we are partners, eh? We'll soon show these children how whist should be played."

His bland acceptance of her being of his generation rather than his son's did not sit well with the lady, and Violet resigned herself to a disagreeable game.

Ralston proved to have an uncanny skill that made her uneasy, even though, at penny points, they played for chicken stakes. Handling the pasteboards without her spectacles she found not to be a problem, for one could hold the cards close to the face on the pretext of keeping them hidden. Montrose, however, was not a skilled practitioner and his foolhardy plays downed them more than once in the first rubber. Violet soon lost all interest in their game.

But not in another. The tables were close together and she was seated with her back to the chair occupied by Lady Redgrave, who had a carrying voice and a topic of conversation far more absorbing than Lord Ralston's continual diatribe on Montrose's clumsiness.

BENTLEY WAS THE RECIPIENT of Beatrix's monologue. Her subject, the coming County Ball, appealed to him far less than the back of Violet's head, just visible over Lady Redgrave's right shoulder. Did that shade of yellow ribbon set off the reddish lights in her shining brown curls, or did their lovely colour need no such embellishment? He was trying to come up with a quotation worthy of such a pleasing combination when he was called to order by his voluble partner.

"What think you, Denville?" she demanded. "Should I dare to dampen my petticoat, or will that mountainous dragon refuse to allow me to leave the house?"

"Leave the house?" he asked. Remembering he was Hildebrand, he twirled his slipping moustache. "Why should she not let you leave? She'd be far more likely to throw you out if you did so. But if you are planning to go outside all wet, you'll no doubt catch your death.''

Lady Redgrave's peal of silvery laughter had a metallic edge. ''I do believe you have not been listening to a word I say. I am speaking of my gown for the County Ball.''

''Pray accept my apologies.'' He bowed his head politely. ''I was concentrating on...on my next play.''

She did not seem to believe him, but apparently decided to let it slide. ''When you see me in that gown, you will be able to concentrate on no one but me. Indeed, the corsage is so short, I shall be living in terror lest I make a sudden movement and my bosom pops right out of it.''

Bentley felt his colour rise. He knew he should say something Hildebrandish, perhaps suggesting that he sincerely hoped to be dancing with her when it happened, but his Bentley Frome tongue somehow tangled with his teeth. Flushing like a greenhead, he pretended to drop a card on the floor while he regained his complexion.

When he straightened, he had an eerie sense of eyes searing into the back of his head. Turning slightly, he met the hot gaze of the lady's husband.

''Two waltzes, remember,'' Lady Redgrave was saying, tapping him on the arm with her hand of cards. ''I shall hold you to that.''

Her high-pitched voice reached easily across the tables, and Bentley couldn't decide which was worse, Lord Redgrave's glare or Violet's thinking he flirted with that abominable female. Perspiration bedewed his upper lip and the moustache slid. He gave it a frantic twirl and Lady Redgrave once more mistook the meaning.

"Two waltzes," she caroled. "You will not regret, Denville, although a high-stepping quadrille might sooner fulfil your desire. Unless. . ." she dropped her voice, but not enough. "Unless you might prefer a private showing."

Lord Redgrave's chair scraped as he rose to his feet and Bentley discovered within himself a Hildebrandish desire to draw the confounded man's cork. He was saved by Lady Hippolyta's sonorous tones changing a dangerous subject.

"You must all," she ordered, "be dressed betimes tomorrow evening, for your servants will wish to ready themselves. The Annual Domestics' Ball is held the same night at Warburton. This is tradition and must be honoured. The Branleigh servants are expected to attend."

Bentley sank back in his chair, as he saw Redgrave resume his seat under the compelling gaze of Lady Hippolyta. He had absolutely no intention of dancing even one waltz under the eyes of that jealous husband, let alone two.

The servants out, and all the guests at the ball. . . Branleigh would be deserted for the whole evening. The County Ball would have to get along without him—after he had at least one dance with Violet. An opportunity to search Branleigh was too great to miss, provided, of course, that Ralston left that oblong case at home.

IN THE GREAT HALL, outside the front drawing-room, Mathilda pretended to dust a table loaded with gim-cracks while she listened at the door. She knew about the Annual Domestics' Ball, for nothing else was being talked of below-stairs. Branleigh would be empty, and she was sure at last that she knew where the diamond was hidden.

She had thoroughly torn apart his lordship's room without finding a trace of it, although she had dis-covered other interesting facets of Ralston's private life. They held no interest for her, however. Men, she knew, would be men. Instead, she had taken to fol-lowing him about the house, dusting here and there, laying fires and clearing ashes. Never had she been so assiduous in her duties.

And it had paid off. She had seen Ralston's fre-quent trips into the library, and had also noted that he was never known to read. Indeed, Hepworth the but-ler maintained that his lordship hadn't the intelli-gence to peruse more than the simplest racing page, and Mathilda agreed. It only remained for Ralston to place the brooch in its cache and to leave the book-room deserted long enough for her light-fingered Norton to locate the treasure.

The door to the front drawing-room had not been completely shut, and Lady Redgrave's shrill voice penetrated into the hall. Two waltzes with "Den-ville," eh? Mathilda's thin lips tightened in satisfaction. Then the Honourable Bentley Frome would be out of the way—and out of luck. Now if Lord Ralston would just go into the library...

The luncheon gong sounded at last and the card-games broke up. Mathilda, invisible as were all servants, continued to dust the same table. Bentley Frome came out among the first, towed along by that brazen hussy, Lady Redgrave. No better than she should be, Mathilda thought virtuously. Master Bentley had best watch his step. Lady Hippolyta waddled out near the end, last except for her nephew. Lord Ralston hung back, and his aunt halted.

"Come along, Ralston," her ladyship ordered imperiously.

His reply was testy. "I'll come when I'm ready."

Lady Hippolyta harrumphed. "Contrary creature," she informed that nice Lady Clarissa Langford, whom she held by the elbow. "Only because I told him to do so. Just like a man."

Mathilda silently agreed. It was a trait she'd often noticed in Norton.

Everyone but Ralston passed on into the dining-room and Mathilda froze, clutching her feather duster. His lordship, a black case in his hands, walked towards the library.

In moments, Mathilda was through the green baize door and running down the servants' hall. Where, oh where, was Norton? She found him in the kitchen, a teacup in his hand, and only just refrained from yanking him from the room by the ear.

Once out in the hall, she sent him hotfooting for the bookroom, already primed as to what he should look for.

NORTON CHECKED his forward momentum at the library door and entered with proper decorum.

Lord Ralston, caught rummaging about with the books on one of the shelves, gave a guilty start.

"What the devil are you doing in here?" he demanded.

Norton ducked his head. "I beg your pardon, your lordship. I was looking for my Lord Denville."

"Well, he's not in here," Ralston snapped. "So get out." He jammed a small black box into his coat pocket as he spoke.

Norton, not altogether dimwitted, hid a suddenly alert glint in his eyes. Could that be the jewellery case containing their diamond brooch? And had he been about to hide it behind those books? It was out of his reach right now, but if his lordship hid it in there regularly... He donned a blank, stupid expression and bowed.

"Yes, my lord," he said, backing away, still bowing. "At once, my lord."

Before he reached the door, it flew open behind him. Lady Hippolyta loomed on the threshold.

"What are you doing in here, Ralston?" she demanded in much the same tone his lordship had used in addressing Norton. "We're waiting for you to take me in to the dining-room."

Ralston glared at her and at Norton, equally furious with both, for her imperious assumption of authority and for the lowly domestic's calm acceptance of it as a well-known fact.

"Come along!" she repeated in a tone that brooked no disobedience. He strode out of the room, Lady Hippolyta billowing after him.

Norton reported back to Mathilda, who waited behind the green baize door. "You 'ad 'im proper pegged, right enough," he congratulated her. "We 'ave 'im now. It's only to bide our time until 'e 'ides that there box again and we find th' bookroom empty."

Mathilda gave him a quick hug and he grinned happily.

"No chance 'e'll suspect us. Not one of your needle-wits, 'is lardship," he added, with a snide reference to Ralston's thickening waistline. "'E'll be just like 'is aunt one o' these days."

Arm in arm, they walked back to the kitchen.

FRUSTRATED IN HIS attempts to get Violet alone, Bentley drifted into the bookroom after lunch. He settled in a wing-chair before the hearth, and gave himself up to day-dreaming about that delightful damsel. He had noted the tell-tale oblong bulge in Ralston's pocket and knew there was nothing to be done at the moment.

Half listening, he heard voices in the hall heralding a general exodus from the card rooms. The billiard-room seemed to be the goal; he heard snatches about a contest. Lord Redgrave, determined to prove himself tops at something, had challenged Montrose.

Better him than me, Bentley thought. *The man would no doubt skewer me on his cue.* As Hildebrand, he almost chuckled, and settled himself more comfortably in the chair, invisible from the rest of the room.

A few minutes later, the door from Ralston's study at the far end of the bookroom opened quietly. There was a mirror over the hearth, and Bentley watched the reflection as his lordship hurried across the room behind him, the black-velvet case in his hand.

Bentley gripped the arms of his chair, white-knuckled. Ralston stopped before one of the bookcases. His lordship reached up to a high shelf, removed a weighty tome, shoved the black case behind it and carefully replaced the volume. Bentley shrank into his wing-chair. If only the man didn't see him...

He didn't. Ralston walked casually back to his study and went in. The moment the door closed, Bentley leaped to his feet. Victory! At last!

He had his hand raised to remove the heavy book when the door from the hall opened and Lady Hippolyta lumbered in. He stepped back, stumbling over a footstool in his haste.

"Ah, Denville," she said. "Surprised you, did I?" She peered about the room. "Alone? What, not hiding one of my maids?"

"Certainly not." Patting and twirling the moustache, he strove for composure. "Merely looking for... for something to read."

She glanced at the shelf he'd been reaching for. "Sermons? I had no idea you had a religious bent." She changed the subject abruptly. "See here, Denville, I've been wanting a word with you. I won't have you turning that innocent chit's head."

Who, me? seemed an inadequate reply and Bentley remained silent. Hildebrand, he thought, would have known just what to say.

She tacked towards a sofa, her skirts luffing like sails in a crosswind. "I like that girl," she said. "Not at all the flibbertigibbet I expected."

Bentley rallied. "Even you must admit she would be wasted on Montrose."

"She's not to be taken in by a lecher like you, however. I told you once to keep away from her. See that you do. Libertine!" She snorted. "Now get out of here. I want my post-prandial nap and this is the only quiet room with a fire that doesn't smoke."

With many grunts and groans, she berthed her great bulk on a sofa, right below the fateful shelf of sermons. After several abortive tries, she managed to hoist her legs up on the cushions and lie down. Spreading a lace handkerchief over her face, she feigned a snore, firmly dismissing him.

There was nothing he could do. He would simply have to return later. But meanwhile, the black case was safe. Since he alone knew where it was, he could afford to wait.

Out in the hall, Bentley came upon the maid, Mathilda, doing some unnecessary dusting near the study door. He hesitated. Housemaids should be out of sight at this hour. Could she be spying on Ralston? And hadn't he better steer her off?

Walking slowly past her, he donned a smug smile and patted his pocket meaningfully. To his relief, she dropped her feather duster with a dismayed gasp and turned to watch him move away. And that, he hoped, would keep the pair of them out of the library should they see Ralston go in.

His pulses pounded as he forced himself to stroll down the hall. At last he could see an end to it. No more potted palms or Oriental vases. Remembering the fire in Lord Redgrave's eyes made him feel more Bentley than Hildebrand. The sooner he had that brooch and was out of Branleigh the better. It was time to go; he was running out of his black hair pomade, the moustache would not stick much longer... and there was Violet.

A knot formed in his stomach. What would she say when he disclosed his real character to her? She'd told him she hated deception and never wished to meet with it again. Would she forgive him when she knew all? The one ray of sunshine in all this murk was that he and not Montrose would have the brooch. He was almost sorry he could not tell him the stone was worthless, robbing him as he meant to do of the girl he loved.

He stopped beside one of the long windows. That was indeed the only ray of sunshine, for none could break through the downpour outside. A long evening of cards and country dances lay ahead. After trying all day to speak to Violet, he was sure she would not stand up with him. He wondered if she had gone to the billiard-room with the rest. He drifted off that way, but failed to find either her or Montrose.

It seemed like hours before the dressing gong sounded and Bentley escaped up to his room. He was just in time to catch Norton, razor in hand, about to rip the lining from an evening coat. The bedchamber had been ransacked.

Striding in, he snatched the razor from Norton's limp fingers. "You're the very devil of a valet!" he remarked. "This is no way to care for your master's clothing!" He shook his head at the cringing ex-footman and folded the razor, putting it in his pocket. "Now I'm certain I'll give you no reference when you leave my service."

When Norton realized he was not to be sliced into portions like a roast fowl by an irate Bentley, he straightened. "I was merely doing a bit o' looking about, as my Mathilda says is called for."

Bentley glanced up from checking his garments for damage. "You're devilishly lucky you hadn't commenced on this start! You're fair and far out searching in here."

Norton raised his eyebrows in a creditable imitation of Hepworth and tried to look down his unfortunate nose. Bentley stood a full hand taller, so he contended himself with a sneer. "Am I now?"

"You are. To save myself further upheavals of my quarters, I reluctantly admit that I do not have that brooch—yet. Now, kindly remove yourself while I dress, and then clean up this wretched mess or you're dismissed.''

Norton swaggered towards the doors. "You ain't gonna dismiss me, Mr. *Denville-Bentley* Frome." He left, and Bentley gave him credit for a good exit line.

At dinner, Lady Hippolyta seized upon Violet again and seated her as far from the dangerous Denville as possible. Bentley's place was flanked by two of the fortyish matrons.

Promised dancing, the ladies had dressed in their semi-best, the gowns they'd worn for the reception the first evening. Bentley once more faced pea-green lustring and wine ribbed silk. The puce satin sat directly in front of him, between Lord Redgrave and Lord Evans. Bentley squinted down the table with a wary eye, looking for their formidable ladies.

Lady Evans, in rose silk that complemented her dark curls, leaned over her cover plate, speaking to Lord Ralston. Lady Redgrave... Bentley gulped. Wearing an almost transparent draping of gauze, in a shade of coquelicot that bordered on brilliant orange, she stood out like a parrot in a flock of sparrows. He breathed a bit easier. This must not be the gown she'd threatened to wear to the County Ball. It had a secure corsage, eliminating the peril of her "popping out" in the middle of a quick step.

His glance passed on to Violet, seated between Lady Hippolyta and Montrose, and rested there, content. Violet had his complete approval. Her demure white orange-blossom crêpe, with a wreath of pink ribbon roses about its low neckline, suited her status as an unmarried maiden to perfection. She was picking nervously at the food on her plate, and even at the distance of the table length, Bentley thought her expression haunted.

He cast his mind back. Of a certainty he had seen her discomposed, but never to such an extent. Something told him that whatever her problem, it had little to do with him. Who, then? Was Montrose pressuring her? His fingers curled into purposeful bunches of fives. He'd plant the fool a facer if it was he who upset Violet.

He wanted to talk to her, perhaps tonight. A niggling unease tugged at him. She had been avoiding him all day; what would she do when he asked her to dance?

He needn't have worried. He hadn't a chance to ask for her hand and spent a miserable evening, first captured by Lady Redgrave and forced to cavort like an idiot under the glowering gaze of her husband, then presented with partners by Lady Hippolyta. Bentley hated country dances, hated hopping and skipping like an awkward stork around the puce satin, and tripping through a contredanse with the pea-green lustring. When he broke away and headed for Violet, he was intercepted by the wine ribbed silk for the final promenade.

Lady Redgrave, only seconds behind her, gave an angry titter, then caught Ralston's arm before the dark-haired Lady Evans could reach him. Perspiration once more loosened the moustache. Bentley determined to end the affair of Letitia's glass brooch this very night and escape from this devilish situation while he still had his whole skin.

He waited in his room until well after midnight. Then, when he was certain all the residents and guests at Branleigh had retired, he started confidently down to the bookroom to retrieve the black case. At the head of the stairs he paused. Were those faint sounds of voices below? He peered over the rail into the darkness of the great hall—and saw a pale line of candlelight seeping from beneath the library door.

Someone else must know of the black box on that bookshelf... Norton? Or robbers? Like Falstaff, Bentley firmly believed "the better part of valour is discretion." He selected a long-handled battle-axe from a display on the wall and crept across the landing. Suddenly, the voices below were raised—a man's, with a woman's nearly hysterical reply. Montrose—and Violet! He dropped the axe and galloped down the remaining steps.

IN THE LIBRARY at Branleigh, the fatal words echoed in Violet's ears. "I now pronounce you man and wife." She had done it. She was married to Montrose. But oh, how far it was from the wedding of her dreams! The clandestine ceremony, the lateness of the hour—and that odd vicar. He could at least have been decently shaven. And the witness he brought must have been picked up at the village tavern! The woman had the disreputable appearance of a barmaid.

Something else bothered her. "Montrose, did we not need a special licence?"

Montrose patted her hand. "Do not concern yourself. I have already given it to the parson."

Violet, whose knowledge of the business side of wedding procedure was vague at best, still felt uneasy.

"But should I not have signed something?"

"No, no. It's all been taken care of."

His manner seemed distinctly evasive. She twisted the handkerchief she had already mangled during the brief ceremony. She had said the vows; she and Monty had been pronounced man and wife. Any questions she might have were not likely to be answered by Montrose, who seemed perfectly satisfied with the result. Oh, if only this bumble-broth could hastily be brought to a conclusion and all set to rights! Meanwhile, she was now wed. Why was she not more relieved?

It had been a difficult decision, resolving to marry Montrose to save herself from seduction by the most dangerous man she'd ever met. She could no longer go on seeing Denville, longing for him to hold her in his arms again and to trace a path down her cheek with his warm lips...while that silly moustache tickled her nose. Really, that moustache had been the only thing which kept her sane, which kept her from falling over a precipice. At least Montrose was clean-shaven.

She faced him, attempting to be reasonable. "We must tell your father who I am. I only agreed to marry you now, Monty, because…because you have been so insistent." She could not tell him the truth!

"But you cannot confess all to my father!" He caught at the hand that wore his signet ring. "Violet, you cannot; I *need* that diamond!"

Not a word about needing *her!* Violet stiffened. "Monty, we can survive without it. You do have a small competence your father cannot take away. Perhaps now that you are wed, he will increase your allowance."

"You don't understand." He seemed near tears. "I must have that diamond. Since I did not marry Clarissa, my aunt will cast me out. I will be without a penny until I gain my inheritance when I am five-and-thirty! The blunt from that brooch will support us until then."

Violet stared at him, aghast. "Monty, you said we would borrow the stone, not keep it to sell! It was only to be held to force your father to turn over your funds!"

Montrose was past dissembling. "He cannot do so. Only my aunt has that power. I told you we'd borrow it only because you would not agree to marry me any other way."

"Monty, you lied to me!"

"I had to! I could not marry you unless I had enough of the ready to be free."

Violet turned away. She had been so certain that marriage to Montrose—to anyone, really—was the only course for her to take in order to survive. Now she knew, irrevocably, that she could not cast her lot with him. But she had! What could she do?

"Violet!" He seized her in his arms and tried to kiss her, catching a corner of her chin as she jerked her head away. His mouth felt wet and hot against her skin and she pounded on his chest with both fists. She didn't want him to touch her. The very thought made her feel ill!

"Let me go! At once!"

"You are my wife!"

He clutched her tighter, and as she struggled to keep her face away from his, the library door burst open.

It was the work of a moment for the tall, moustached man who entered to grab the seat of Montrose's breeches in one hand and the slack of his collar with the other and to throw him bodily out into the hall. He closed the door, turned the key in the lock and dusted his hands on his satin evening inexpressibles.

"I collect," he remarked conversationally, "that meets with your approval."

Violet smoothed her disordered hair and strove to regain her composure. "I...yes, I—I find Montrose...that is, we do not suit."

"I should think not. Now, on the other hand, you and I do."

She stared at him. What could he mean? Surely, he'd not offer her a *carte blanche!*

"You must know how I feel," he went on diffidently. "Oh, lord, how shall I say it? As King Lear once remarked, 'I fear I am not in my perfect mind.'

Violet, the hour has come for truth between us. 'Love, and a cough, cannot be hid.'"

Love! She gasped, her world rocking. "You . . . my lord Denville, you cannot!"

"Oh, to the devil with Denville!" His voice shook. "Violet, tell me you are not indifferent to me."

"You are married! And I—"

He reached for his moustache, and for a wild moment she thought he would tear it off. She started to scream.

Another scream came from without. A despairing howl, accompanied by bumps and bangs and ending in a cataclysmic crash amid shattering glass and china.

CHAPTER NINE

NORTON LAY on the stone floor, blinking in the darkness of the great hall, and wondered what had happened to him. His questing hands informed him that he was surrounded by debris—splintered table legs, bits of ornamental figurines, shards of china and glass. Flowers—roses and lilies—lay scattered over his chest and his breeches were soaked with the water from their broken bowl. He was vaguely surprised to find he was not dead. Someone, somewhere beside him, groaned.

His mind gradually began to clear and he remembered. One minute he had been sneaking quietly down from his attic room and had reached the main staircase. The next, he tripped on something and plummeted, heels over ears, into the depths and cannoned into a solid body in the hall. He sat up, still groggy, and began to count his arms and legs, while the world filled with shouting people waving candles.

One of the footmen was lighting the hall sconces with a taper, and they illuminated a scene of devastation. His companion, in a skidding plunge across the hall from the foot of the stairs, had demolished an occasional table loaded with gimcracks before he finished up against a chest by the library door. Norton, with the battle-axe he'd tripped over running a poor second, had accounted for another, and it now lay in bits about him.

Still hurriedly belting a wine velvet dressing-gown that bore a pattern of orange peonies, Lord Ralston stood over them, glaring like a basilisk and waving a pistol.

"What the devil," he demanded, "do you two think you're doing?"

Norton had by now decided he was all in one piece. He struggled painfully to his feet and discovered that the other victim was Mr. Montrose. Hepworth, he noted with no little anxiety, held a shotgun aimed at his chest, obviously feeling that defence of the household came under the heading of butler's duties.

"I can explain everything!" he yelped.

INSIDE THE LIBRARY, Bentley froze, Violet still in his arms. Good God, that racket would bring everyone in the house into the hall, and Violet must not be caught here with a man—a married man and a supposedly gazetted rake! He shoved her behind the heavy floor-length draperies of the nearest window.

"For Lord's sake, stay there!" he whispered. "I'm going to see what it is, and when the coast is clear, I'll come back for you."

She nodded mutely and pulled in her skirts and her toes. Satisfied that no one could see her, he dropped a quick kiss on her forehead, gave her a reassuring hug and let himself out into the maelstrom in the hall.

Montrose sat on the floor looking dazed, his head resting against a chest by the bookroom door. He was surrounded by broken china and pieces of what had once been an occasional table or two. Bentley's new valet, dripping flowers and water, stood in the centre of a group attired in dressing gowns and nightcaps. Hepworth, he noted with approval, held a shotgun pointed at Norton's chest in a threatening manner. Even without his spectacles, he could see that the stone-paved floor of the hall looked as though a berserk bull had wandered through. Bentley leaned back against the wall with folded arms, prepared to be entertained. Norton did not fail him.

The ex-footman had by now assembled the wits that had temporarily parted company with his meagre brain.

"Robbers!" he shouted. "I 'eard them prowling about down 'ere and when I run to apprehend the varmints, one of them sticks that there battle-axe between me legs and up-ends me!"

At this, the ladies of the house, who had collected on the landing above, began to shriek. Cries of "Robbers! Thieves! Murderers!" echoed through the hall. Footmen were sent to search the house, women scuttled to secure their jewel cases and Hepworth, still cradling his shotgun, trod into his pantry with less than his usually majestic dignity to count the Branleigh silver. Montrose had melted away.

In the hall, only Bentley, Norton and Ralston remained, and up on the landing, a mountain of mauve satin negligée. Lady Hippolyta, awesome *en dés-*

habillé without her confining stays, looked down at them.

"Fustian," she pronounced. A pudgy finger pointed at Bentley, who had lacked the sense to disappear with Montrose. "What are you doing down there, Denville? Still dressed, too. Why weren't you in bed like an honest man?"

Norton fixed him with a jaundiced eye. "Aye, why ain't yer?"

Trapped, Bentley pushed away from the wall, his mind on protecting Violet hidden in the library. "Couldn't sleep," he explained, forcing an insouciant calm. "I came down for a book to read. Possibly," he added brightly, "It was I Norton heard. I didn't realize the tumult that would result."

The ex-footman sneered, about to say something, and changed his mind.

Ralston picked up the battle-axe thoughtfully and leaned it against the wall where Bentley had been standing. "I collect this must have fallen from its rack onto the stairs. It has hung there for a century or more and no doubt the bracket that held it became loosened." He turned coldly to Norton. "You must have sustained some injury. You could not have so demolished my hall otherwise. I suggest you go at once to the housekeeper and request an embrocation for your bruises."

Norton, already suspecting a number of nasty flesh-wounds in the area of his posterior, headed for the green baize doors leading to the servants' hall, and Ralston's eye returned to Bentley.

"Good night," he said pointedly.

There seemed no way to outwait the man, so Bentley started reluctantly up the stairs. He'd have to come back for Violet.

Lady Hippolyta had already retired. At the landing, he looked down and to his horror saw Ralston walk into the library. His stomach sank and he prayed that Violet was still out of sight behind the draperies. He paused, ears straining, but heard no voices. Should he go back? Say he had forgot his book? He was halfway down the flight when Ralston came out, tucking something into the pocket of his deplorable dressing-gown.

Bentley scrambled back up the stairs and shrank down behind a large chest on the wide landing. Ralston passed by without seeing him. As soon as the man was safely away, Bentley charged down again and into the library. He pulled the draperies aside.

Violet was gone.

VIOLET HAD CLUNG to a fold of the velvet drapery behind which she hid, listening to the tumult in the hall outside. Voices shouted, footsteps rang on the paving, and women shrieked in the distance. Plainly, something of import had occurred, but in no way could it equal the chaos within herself.

Denville had fallen in love with her. And, she had to confess, so had she with him. It was impossible! A hopeless impasse! She must get away from him at once. But she could not live with Montrose, as she might have done had he not lied to her. Could a marriage be annulled? She had no idea how.

Nor could she be kept by a married man. She knew all about the dangers of forbidden fruit, but try though she did, she couldn't convince herself that Denville was other than the one man she desired....

It had been silent in the hall for several minutes, she realized finally. Was the crisis, whatever it was, passed? Why did Denville not return? She heard the latch click and started out, stopping just in time. That was not Denville she saw through a crack in the draperies. He had been garbed in a gentleman's correct evening attire, and although she hadn't her spectacles, she could see the newcomer wore a dazzlingly flowered dressing-gown. She shrank back and watched.

In the flickering light from the candelabra that had been left burning from her meeting with Montrose, she recognized Lord Ralston. He went directly to one of the bookcases on the opposite wall and reached unerringly for a thick volume on one of the upper shelves.

Violet squinted, trying to see. What was he doing? He took something from behind the book and hesitated, weighing it in his hand as though coming to a decision. It looked like a flattish black jewellery case. About to return it to its hiding-place, he apparently changed his mind and replaced the book instead. As he left the room, she saw him tuck the box into a pocket of his dressing-gown.

Violet stood where she was, trembling with excitement. It *was* a jewellery case, for certain! Now she knew where the Denville diamond was hidden when Lord Ralston did not carry it on his person. She *knew*, and she could get it the next time Ralston put it away. She could hand it to Montrose, and maybe he would free her from her hasty vows.

But she'd not be free from Denville, who might return at any moment. Slipping from behind the draperies, she ran across the room to Ralston's study and waited, crouched behind his desk, until all sounds of Denville's hunting her in the library next door ceased.

Then, quickly, she ran up the back stairs to her room and locked the door. She lay awake in terror until dawn, but Montrose made no attempt to enter her room.

VIOLET CAME DOWN very early for breakfast, hoping to avoid a meeting with either of the other participants in the momentous occurrences in the library the night before. She was not in luck. She had hardly filled her plate at the sideboard when Montrose came in and fairly pounced on her, full of apologies.

He caught her hands, nearly spilling her kippers and toast onto the carpet. "My dearest," he begged, "forgive me. I quite lost my head. I do not know what got into me!"

Violet pried his fingers loose and armed herself with a fork. "Monty, pray let me go. This . . . this is not the time or place to settle matters between us. Anyone may come in!"

"I don't care. Violet, say I am forgiven. I acted the boor—the cad! Only my great love caused me to use you in so ungentlemanly a fashion."

"If you mean by seizing and forcing yourself upon a defenceless female even though you . . . you had the right, your actions were indeed ungentlemanly. But you also lied to me. That is what I find unforgivable."

"Violet, you *must* forgive me; how else can we begin our married life?" He caught at her hands again and she dodged away, placing her endangered plate on the table.

"Monty, listen to me. I am sorry, but I am not going through with this marriage. I cannot!"

"Violet!"

She faced him, her back to the sideboard for support. "I have thought it all over, Monty, and I have decided we will not suit." Denville's words came back to her and she felt her face flush. "No, Monty, you and I will not suit." Of that, she was certain. Of herself and Denville—she could only wish they had never met.

Monty was clinging to her hands, shaking them up and down. "You cannot mean that! Dearest Violet, you promised!"

She pulled free and added the fork to her abandoned plate. Monty's stricken expression roused all her feelings of guilt.

"I promised to help you *borrow* that brooch, and you promised not to keep it. I will still help you do that, but we must now apply to Lady Hippolyta to grant your funds. She will decide whether to return the brooch to your father. My only concern is that you release me immediately from the foolish vows I made last night.''

''I don't know how such an unworthy thought entered my head. I only wanted my fortune so badly so that we might be properly wed. Say we will, Violet, my love!''

She shook her head firmly. ''You must rid yourself of that idea. I cannot live with you.''

''Violet, I want you.''

''You can't have me.''

''Can't I?'' His expression changed. ''I daresay I need not look far for the reason!'' His brows drew together in a black look that gave him a startling resemblance to his father. ''Denville!''

Violet gasped, spinning around. ''Where?''

''I don't know where that blasted libertine is now, but I know where he has been. In the garden with you—and in the library last night!''

She opened her mouth, about to deny all, and realized that he was quite right. He didn't know about the scene in her bedchamber, but she didn't feel it necessary to tell him.

''And in m'father's wardrobe. That you have never explained.''

''It was all your fault!'' She rounded on him, grasping at an excuse to turn the tables. ''You sneaked in and frightened me—after I ordered you not to try! I told you I would take care of it, and I might have found the brooch that very night instead of having to cope with both you and Denville.''

"Yes," he agreed nastily. "I've seen you coping with Denville.''

Violet felt the colour rush to her cheeks and saw by his face that he had witnessed it.

His mouth became set in a thin, bitter line. "Then my father is right. I see. That is why you're crying off—you are having an affair with a married man!''

Violet couldn't think of words strong enough to voice her indignation. Her bosom heaved like a heroine's in a melodrama and her tongue cleaved to the roof of her mouth in her fury.

Montrose misinterpreted her silence. "So I have found you out!" he exclaimed. "Wanton woman, you may consider our marriage at an end!" He turned—on his heel, she was sure—and stalked from the room.

You'll be sorry, she thought irrelevantly. *You have forgot to eat your breakfast.* She looked down at her own plate, wondering how she could be hungry at such a climactic moment. If Montrose spread his story about her and Denville, her reputation would be ruined. She ought to have run after him and denied everything, but it was too late now. Too late for anything. Despite what he had just said, Montrose and she were well and truly married and what was she going to do?

It was indeed the proverbial ill wind, she mused. At least now she could forget that dratted diamond. She hadn't told him of the black box in the bookcase, and she wasn't about to do so. If he discovered it on his own, she hoped he'd choke on it. She sat down and began to eat her cold kippers and toast.

VIOLET SPENT a most difficult day. Ever conscious of Montrose's accusations, she strove to avoid the dangerous Earl of Denville. She was miserably aware that her feelings for him were far from those of friendship, and knowing that he felt the same compounded her agony. Denville, however, appeared determined to talk to her and seemed to be laying in wait at every turning. Only constant vigilance on her part kept her out of his way. Montrose, on the other hand, developed a tendency to stiffen alarmingly on seeing her, his face scarlet and his nose twitching like an infuriated rabbit.

Only one thought kept her from turning tail and running away and that was of Simpson. As a gesture of appreciation, Clarissa had provided her loyal abigail with one of her own gowns, the first truly elegant toilette the woman had ever owned. Though neither of them thought they would stay at Branleigh so long, now Simpson could wear the gown to the Annual Domestics' Ball. How could she deprive Simpy of such a treat, after receiving the woman's support and protection during this odious masquerade? Indeed, she could not be so selfish.

Attempting to escape into the ladies' parlour upstairs, she ran straight into Lady Hippolyta, who collared her at once.

"I want to talk to you, young lady."

"Yes, ma'am." Caught, her heart pounding, Violet sank into a chair opposite the sofa that was nearly covered by Lady Hippolyta and her voluminous skirts.

"I like you," said her ladyship. "You're no milk-and-water miss, nor are you a hoyden. Now that I've met you again, I'm beginning to think you'll be wasted on my nincompoop of a great-nevvy." With the piercing lance of her gaze, she fixed Violet to the chair. "But no good comes of an interest in a married man."

Oh, dear God, Violet thought. *Have I been so obvious? First Montrose and now Lady Hippolyta.* She felt her cheeks flame and rushed into a stammered disavowal.

"No, no, ma'am. It—it is not Denville. It was just that I—I knew his brother."

"Indeed." Her ladyship's scepticism could be sliced with a knife and served up. "From what I've heard of Mr. Bentley Frome, he's a ginger-hackled long-shanks. Not all the crack like Denville."

Violet's quick defence of her knight was genuine. "Mr. Frome is a gentleman! All that is honourable and ... and kind!"

"Is he now? I daresay he's not a patch on Denville." The dowager looked at her closely. "Too bad Denville has already fallen into parson's mousetrap. Too bad, indeed. He'd have been just the man for you."

Agreeing all too readily, Violet held her tongue.

Lady Hippo sat back and the sofa gave an alarming creak. "However." She slapped her hands down on her roly-poly knees. "You're better off with a twiddly fribble like Montrose than with accepting a *carte blanche* from Denville, which is what I imagine he has in mind."

Violet nearly choked. So that was what they were all thinking! Well, was it not what she herself feared?

Her ladyship was not done. She reached out a chubby hand and patted Violet's wrist. "I hope you've not been blinded like a silly Bath miss by his elegant appearance and glamorous reputation. Not that I wouldn't understand, my dear. If I were twenty years younger, I'd be tempted to cast sheep's eyes at him myself. But he's not for a young girl," she said sternly. "Leave him to the matrons who understand the rules of the games he plays."

In good earnest, Violet assured her that she meant to do just that.

"Ah," said Lady Hippolyta, satisfied. "Then, my dear Clarissa, we must puff off your betrothal to Montrose at once. I have already written out announcements for the *Morning Post* and the *Gazette*. They shall go tomorrow. I have decided the best time for the ceremony would be September, as a fitting beginning for the Little Season. It will, of course, take place at Branleigh."

Violet opened her mouth to inform the formidable old lady that it was too late, but she couldn't make herself heard. Lady Hippolyta rolled on, causing Violet to feel like a lagging hound being ridden over by a boisterous huntsman. Her ladyship looked forward to staging her god-daughter's wedding and she was in full cry. Violet expected her, any moment, to shout, "View haloo, yoicks and tally-ho!"

"I shall have the banns published in our local church these next three successive Sundays, right after the Second Lesson. Your father may wish to have you wed in St. George's, but I think it will be best to have it here in our chapel at Branleigh, where I can manage the whole affair. It is inconvenient that your home is in another parish, for that means the banns must be proclaimed there as well, with proof in the form of a certificate supplied to our curate. I shall see to that—"

"But Lady Hippo...Hippolyta—" Violet interrupted as her ladyship paused to draw breath. "Really, you must not—"

"Don't give another thought to the arrangements. I have planned it all. Wait," she said, as Violet rose to her feet in desperation, "I have something here for you. A betrothal gift."

She dug into the reticule that lay in her lap, and extracted a ring set with the largest ruby Violet had ever seen. "This is for you. Left to me out of the Ralston family jewels," she explained hastily. "Mine to dispose of, not as an heirloom."

"No! Oh, no!" Violet thrust back the hand holding the fabulous gem. "I cannot!" Not even if she truly were Clarissa could she accept such a gift, not when she meant to flee from Branleigh and from Montrose. "Please, my lady. You must keep it—until the ceremony," she added on a flash of genius. "Only when the marriage is official will I have the right to own such a precious jewel." Suddenly, unaccountably, tears filled her eyes. "You are too good!" she exclaimed, and fled from the room.

Lady Hippolyta gazed after her thoughtfully. "Well, well," she remarked to the empty room.

THE DRESSING GONG sounded as Violet hesitated in the hall. She ran along the corridor to her bedchamber and stopped in the doorway, her eyes wide.

Simpson had laid out Clarissa's ball gown, spreading the skirts over the coverlet of her bed. Violet walked over slowly, still not believing she'd be allowed to wear the fairy-tale creation. But she would! And tonight. One last leaf for her book of memories.

She lifted the gown tenderly and held it in front of her as she gazed at her image in the long glass beside her dressing-table. The white sarcenet, trimmed with blond lace, pink satin roses and knots of silver ribbon, floated like a cloud over the underdress of rose pink satin. Cut very low, the bodice was ornamented in the new French style, with a wreath of clustered rosebuds outlining the extremely high waistline. Tiny puffed sleeves stopped at the level of the neckline, where they were tied with knots of silver ribbon and dotted with satin roses. The skirt ended in a deep, rich flounce of lace, topped with a *rouleau* of the rose satin and decorated with more roses and ribbon knots.

The headdress was a Kent toque, of pale pink Parisian gauze edged with matching satin roses and silver ribbon. The soft plume of snowy ostrich feathers curled around to brush her cheek.

Violet drew a deep breath. "'Tomorrow, do thy worst,'" she quoted aloud, "'for I have liv'd to-day.'" Or, I will tonight, she amended to herself.

A light tap on the door announced the entrance of Simpson, and Violet gave herself up to the moment.

THE HONOURABLE Bentley Frome paced the hall, complete to a shade in his faultless long-tailed coat, white waistcoat, frilled shirt, black satin knee-breeches and striped silk stockings. He was not happy. All in all, he felt a trifle discouraged. Not only had the oblong bulge been in Lord Ralston's coat pocket all day, but also Violet had been avoiding him as though he'd acquired leprosy.

If Ralston would only hide the black jewel case, this evening when Branleigh was deserted Bentley could nip back from the ball and collect Letitia's brooch from behind the book in the library. A quick dash to Frome to give it to Letitia and wash the pomade from his hair, and he could return for Violet as himself. If! He sighed. When he disclosed the fact that he had been deceiving her all these days, she might never wish to see him again.

The male half of the party began to assemble in the great hall, and Lord Ralston came down the stairs. Eagerly, Bentley ran his eyes over the man's smooth-fitting coat, for "hope springs eternal in the human breast." His hope was doomed to extinction. The sharp edges of the black box showed clearly in one of his lordship's pockets.

"Oh, the devil," Bentley muttered, frustrated.

Ralston caught him staring and met his gaze. Something of the odd unease that Bentley had noticed that first evening flickered across his lordship's features. Before Bentley could decide if it was guilt, fear or merely distaste, a bevy of ladies, resplendent in their full-dress finery, came down the stairs.

In the ensuing commotion of chatter and admiration, Bentley saw Ralston slip quietly into the library, then a minute or so later, come out again, smiling blandly on one and all. His garments were now correctly sleek and smooth; the bulge in his pocket was gone.

Bentley's spirits rose with a bound. He caught one of the footmen, drew him aside and slipped a half-crown into his hand.

"Not a word," he whispered, "but have my team and curricle brought round to the side door as quick as may be."

As the man left on his errand, a sudden silence fell on the company in the hall. Bentley turned to see what was the matter. All eyes were riveted on the staircase, down which Lady Redgrave made her impressive entrance.

Her gown was all she had claimed. Her damped petticoat clung to her legs as she descended, and its transparency made a travesty of the virginal white of her gauze skirt. Her stays pushed her bosom so high that the lace edging at the impossibly low-cut neckline utterly failed to conceal it. Pop out when she danced, indeed! The popping had already been done.

After one horrified glance, Bentley bolted for the side door, praying she had not seen him. He waited, cowering in the shadows, until his curricle arrived, and drove off to Warburton Castle more determined than ever to shake the dust of the County Ball—and Branleigh—from his heels at the very first opportunity.

THE ANNUAL Domestics' Ball, held that same night, also took place at Warburton Castle, in a gigantic hall that had once barracked the veritable army needed to protect the castle in medieval times. While the Quality danced in the elegant ballroom in the main building, their servants would frolic less than a quarter of a mile away.

Mathilda, already dressed in her very best gown, watched the assembling of the glittering crowd from behind the green baize doors of Branleigh with the rest of the maids. While they exclaimed in undertones over the various brilliantly coloured toilettes of the ladies, Mathilda's eyes were on the somber figure of Lord Ralston. She saw him surreptitiously enter the library and come out again, confident and cheery, and she hadn't a doubt as to what he had done.

Slipping away, she collared Norton.

"'E's done it," she hissed in his ear. "Soon as they all go, you get in that there bookroom and find that black box of 'is."

Norton closed his eyes, called up the scene in the library and nodded. "I got it. I remembers which shelf and all."

The maids returned from the baize doors, milling about in the servants' hall, and Hepworth tried to call them to order.

"The Family and guests have left. All of you proceed to the stable-yard," he ordered. "The carriages are waiting to take us to Warburton. Soon's I lock up, we'll be off."

Under cover of the giggling and squealing of the younger domestics, Norton hurried into the great hall. At the library door he was stopped by Hepworth, and his stomach dropped to his knees.

"Ah," said Hepworth. "There's still your master's night-rail to be laid out, eh? Nip up there like a good lad. I'll just be bolting the front door."

Norton's stomach slowly stabilized, leaving his knees wobbly. He managed to murmur, "Yes, sir. At once, sir," to Hepworth's receding back. Then he entered the sanctum of the Denville diamond.

He went straight to the bookshelf, found the correct volume after some difficulty, and finally clasped the black box in his hands. Hepworth called to him to hurry and he stuck it quickly into his pocket.

There'd be no need to do for Master Bentley Frome any longer. If he had what he thought, he and his Mathilda would be long gone this very night.

He floated out on a rosy cloud to join the butler and accompany him to the coach yard.

CHAPTER TEN

IN THE STABLE YARD, the Branleigh domestics milled about the coaches that were to take them to Warburton Castle. Mathilda hung back, waiting eagerly for Norton, and ran to meet him when he came out. But she couldn't ask about the diamond in front of Hepworth. The butler locked the huge kitchen doors and herded them both back towards the carriages with all the irritability of a harried sheepdog after a pair of recalcitrant stragglers. Norton hadn't a chance to speak.

"Just as if the old stiff-rump 'adn't been 'olding us waiting out 'ere for near an 'our, what with all 'is 'aving to see to the locking up," Mathilda grumbled. "Well?"

Norton, conscious of a possible audience, replied silently, but with so many winks, grimaces and pats at his pocket that Mathilda pretended to bump into him, delivering a sharp kick to his shin in the process.

It wasn't until the coach they rode in disgorged its excited passengers in the castle courtyard that they were able to find a corner in which to be alone. Huddled with their backs to the yard, in the dim glow of light cast by one of the flambeaus, they felt it safe to steal a look at the Denville Diamond. Norton took the black case from his pocket and, holding his breath, opened it and looked inside.

The next moment, he gave an anguished howl.

Mathilda grabbed the case. "What is it? Is it gone?"

"Nothing but a damned pack o'cards in 'ere!" With an inarticulate cry, he threw the case to the ground.

Mathilda scooped it up, staring at it. "I don't understand. This is the right box."

Norton snorted. "Plain as a pikestaff, init? 'E's on to us and playing us for a pair o' gowks!"

She gripped his arm, suddenly fearful. "'Is lordship suspects us? 'E knows? Then that there case was put in behind those books as a trap! Mr. Bentley 'as gone and betrayed us!"

He stared at her. She was right. Already he was a known thief, albeit an unsuccessful one. He always had bad luck. But that was going to change, by God. He compressed his lips and squared his shoulders. "I'm going back to Branleigh 'ere and now, and I'll find that blasted diamond if I 'as to tear the place down!"

Mathilda felt a surge of admiration for this man of action, but she was practical. "You're going, all right and tight, but you're going to put that there box back where you found it." She bent to gather up the scattered cards that had fallen out on the paving stones. "No need to let 'im know 'e's diddled us."

She replaced the cards in the black case and handed it to him. "We go on just like nothing 'as 'appened, innocent as a pair o' turtle doves. When 'e sees 'is box is still there, 'e'll be lulled, see. Then we watch 'im while 'e's all unsuspecting.''

Norton looked at the box in his hands. "''Ow do I get back? The carriages is all 'ere.''

"You walk.'' She gave him a shove. "Can't be more'n two or three mile.''

He opened his mouth, met her eye and heaved a groan of resignation. At least it wasn't raining—at the moment.

INSIDE THE CASTLE, Violet stood spellbound on the edge of the dance floor in the huge ballroom, drinking in the glittering candlelight, the beautiful gowns, the sounds of musicians tuning their instruments above the hubbub of conversation. She drew in a deep breath, savouring the mingled scents of beeswax candles, flowers and the lavish perfumes of the ladies and gentlemen.

Truly, Warburton Castle had outdone itself. Hundreds of candles blazed in a magnificent chandelier, its lustres sparkling like myriad diamonds. In imitation of Lady Weldon, who had created the style, the room was decorated as a fanciful tent, with ell after ell of pink calico suspended from the central point above the chandelier to the cornices of the twelve long windows on each side wall. Garlands of greenery, hanging baskets of ferns, potted palm trees and flowery bouquets adorned the walls.

Violet longed to take her spectacles from Clarissa's fancy evening reticule so that she could really see it.

Even gazing at it all as though through a fog, she felt transported, and the words of Byron sang in her mind: "On with the dance! let joy be unconfined." She hoped no one would guess how she trembled inside. She must remain calm! Lady Clarissa had attended many balls fully as grand as this.

And in equally lovely gowns. She smoothed her sarcenet skirt, conscious of the rose-pink satin blushing through the thin material, and felt the soft colour repeated in her cheeks, lent by her excitement. Denville had once likened her to Queen Titania.... What would he quote to her tonight if she dared to dance with him?

Promptly at ten o'clock, the orchestra struck up the opening bars of a country dance and sets began to form. Her tremble became a shiver of anticipation. Would Denville ask to stand up with her? And should she refuse? It would be the last time...

He was across the wide room, his eyes searching the crowd. She stood very still, suddenly not wanting to be alone, and looked about for the other ladies of their party. Lady Hippolyta sat on a sofa nearby and she went to stand behind her.

Violet had ridden over with Lady Hippolyta and hadn't seen Lady Beatrix Redgrave—until now. She stared, her eyes wide. Clarissa had told her of seeing such gowns on very fast females, but surely—oh, the woman would not dare to attempt a twirl or a quickstep! But there, she was heading for Denville! Violet stifled a giggle as he hastily escaped behind a cluster of gentlemen.

She was so occupied with her thoughts that she heard only the end of an on dit being related with great delight to Lady Hippolyta. The purple-turbaned matron who was speaking emphasized each phrase with a tap of her fan on her ladyship's massive arm.

"... on the Great North Road. At an inn less than ten miles from Gretna Green. Eating breakfast as cool as you please, you must know, the butter not melting in their mouths, and a coach and four awaiting them outside in the yard!"

"Oh, your informant was sadly mistaken." Lady Hippolyta brushed away the fan with an annoyed gesture.

"But it is true! My friend knows them both well. It was Sir Edward Moore, and his companion was no other than Lady Clarissa Langford. They have eloped!"

"That cannot be," said the dowager, shaking her head. "Why, the girl is right here." She turned ponderously, but, like Cinderella hearing the clock strike the fatal hour of midnight, Violet had fled.

VIOLET PUSHED HER WAY through the crowd, and ran down corridors until she found a door leading outside. Her only conscious thought was to escape, to get back to Branleigh and leave a message for the faithful Simpson, warning her that she must post off to Dover at once and board the next packet to France. Violet prayed she had enough money to pay her own coach fare to a small inn somewhere, where she might put up cheaply until she could decide what to do next. She certainly could not go back to Clarissa's home after the part she had taken in concealing her cousin's elopement. The Marquis of Scofield would be wild with fury over the deceit of his only daughter.

What could she do? Certainly not go to Montrose, not after that horrendous scene in the library. Not after the way he had acted! She pushed away the memory of how Denville acted. If only it was his brother who had so disrupted her life!

Her running feet had carried her to the stable yard and she stood in the darkness, nonplussed. She had to return to Branleigh, but it must be several miles away—and she was uncertain even of the direction.

BACK IN THE BALLROOM, Bentley encountered troubles of his own, receiving a nasty shock the moment he entered the wide doors. There, not ten paces from him, easily within his limited vision, stood one of Hildebrand's oldest friends. He didn't need the spectacles that rested in his pocket to identify Sir John Woods.

He backed cautiously away, seeking shelter among a bevy of chaperons who had collected by the door. This was the very devil! He'd forgot the man had an estate in this county. From a distance, to a casual acquaintance, he could possibly pass as Hildebrand. But not at any distance could he fool the bluff, red-faced Sir John, who knew Bentley well. He could already hear the man exposing the hoax with hearty guffaws.

The matrons, apparently seeing a friend, moved off in a group, exposing Bentley to the room. Sir John faded from his thoughts as he saw Lady Beatrix Redgrave, in all the glory of her infamous gown, bearing down on him with the fell purpose of dragging him into one of the sets already being made up.

He dove after the crowd of matrons, intending to ask one of them to stand up with him instead, remembered Sir John and shrank behind a veritable zareba of potted palms in the far corner of the ballroom. With thudding pulse he settled down on the sharp edge of one of the pots and watched the frustrated Lady Redgrave search for him.

Minutes passed in comparative peace while he tried to decide what to do. He had meant to stay only long enough to make sure that Ralston knew he was among those present, and thus allay any suspicion his lordship might have that Lord Denville had stayed behind to steal back the brooch. That no longer mattered, for life had become too dangerous at Warburton Castle.

It became more so.

A mighty clap on the back shot him out of the palms into the centre of the country dance now forming.

"Bentley! Isn't that you? I thought so. What the devil are you up to?"

Bentley gasped, trying to recover his wind.

"I say," Sir John went on, in a voice meant to carry across a hunting field. "That moustache! Outside of enough! Are you pretending to be Denville?"

Bentley tried to shush him. "Quiet, man! Someone will hear." Fortunately, they were near the orchestra, which was playing a rousing air with gusto.

"Never knew you to be up to tricks," Sir John bellowed happily. "I'll lay you odds Denville put you up to this. What's his game, eh? Let me in on it. I'll back you, whatever the lark you're staging."

"Only keep quiet," Bentley pleaded, yanking him back behind the palms. "Confound it, Sir John, don't give me away!"

"Give you away?" Sir John bent over, his finger to his lips. "Who, me? Bless you, my boy, I am no marplot!"

Bentley pushed the slipping moustache back into place, absently twirling it, and Sir John crowed with delight.

"But tell me, when is the great dénouement to come off? I must not miss it."

"Not for a while yet. Not for at least an hour. Just go away—over there, by that, ah, rosebush bouquet and wait. You will see all." *All you are going to see,* he added to himself. *I hope!*

Sir John started off, chortling, then came back. "I say, this is too good to keep."

"Keep it!" Bentley almost howled.

"I'll only let on to a few pals, that's all. And tell them to keep mum."

Bentley groaned as Sir John, the image of a man with a secret, tip-toed ostentatiously away, collaring a friend as he went. *Thank God,* Bentley thought, *I had the foresight to arrange for my curricle to be on hand!*

He was going to need a quick escape, a great deal quicker than he had planned. If he knew Sir John— and he did!—the story should reach Ralston's ears in approximately ten minutes. He headed for the door at a near run. Back to Branleigh at once, a trip into the library to get that brooch and then leave a note for Lady Hippolyta, requesting that his baggage be sent home, as he had been called away urgently. Letitia's baby would make a splendid excuse.

And he'd best make good time. If Ralston caught up with him before his lordship's rage cooled, he'd likely call him out, or at the very least take after him with that battle-axe which hung once more at the landing over the stairs. The man would not care for being the butt of a hoax before his acid-tongued aunt.

Bentley reached the carriage house and hastily hitched up his team. Actually, the only change in his plans was his speedier departure... but it would have been nice could he have had one waltz with Violet....

LADY HIPPOLYTA was in ault. Gowned in her favourite lilac satin, her head a fountain of nodding purple ostrich-plumes sprouting from a jeweled silk-and-velvet turban that matched her robe, she had spent the early evening spread across a puff-pillowed settee provided for her by a thoughtful hostess. Her eyes snapped with malicious glee as she watched Denville dodging Beatrix Redgrave. The sight of the man crouching behind the potted palms quite made her evening, but her nephew Ralston, gamboling about Lady Redgrave like a lovesick, middle-aged faun during the next dance, ran Denville's antics a close second.

And now, to top all, here was this affair of the elopement of Lady Clarissa. Seen on the road to Gretna Green—and at the same time visiting at Branleigh? So she had been harbouring an impostor! No wonder the deceitful minx had fled the ballroom as if a pack of hounds were at her heels. She must have heard that gossip-monger's tale. Only if guilty would she flee before she was questioned.

One of Denville's bits of muslin, out to hoax them all, she supposed. And where was the harm? A grudging smile tugged at her lips. Drat it, she *liked* the girl. Game as a pebble, like she herself in the old days. And far too good for a milksop like Montrose. She shrugged. No doubt this was all for the best, for now she wouldn't have to beggar them all by parting with Montrose's chunk of funds when he married.

As Lady Hippolyta looked about for further diversion, her questing eye hit on Lady Evans, who stood by the dance floor glowering as Beatrix Redgrave and Ralston pranced and twirled down the line. The jewels decorating Lady Evans' own noticeable expanse of bosom were patently false. Lady Hippolyta happened to know from her younger days that there were no such gems in the Evans coffers, nor could his present lordship afford such extravagance.

Looking at jewellery brought her thoughts to that aggravating diamond that was causing Ralston to get so above himself. She never had managed to complete her search of his bedchamber. She eyed him thoughtfully as he skipped through a quick-step, his eyes glued to Beatrix Redgrave's décolletage. He would be occupied for some time. And how fortunate that the Annual Domestics' Ball was held here in this same castle. She had only to send word to her coachman to bring her carriage round to the door and she could be back in Branleigh, free to explore as she wished, in less than an hour.

She caught the sleeve of a passing footman.

As BENTLEY led his equipage out into the courtyard, Violet rushed to his side, her skirts caught up in one hand. Her soft hair trailed about her face, pale in the light from the flambeaus, and her ostrich plumes sagged over her shoulders.

"Denville!" she cried. "Oh, Denville!"

Bentley dropped the reins he held and caught her in his arms. "Good God!" he exclaimed. "What has happened?"

She pulled away and patted ineffectually at her hair, trying for composure. "Please, Denville, you must help me."

"Anything in my power," he assured her. "Wait a moment." He trotted after his straying horses and retrieved them. "Now tell me what you wish me to do. But make it quick," he added. "I am in a bit of a hurry."

"Denville!" she exclaimed tragically. "I must return to Branleigh at once!"

"Ah, in that case, nothing simpler. I am on my way there this moment. Here, let me help you." Boosting her into the curricle, he climbed up beside her and wasted no time in springing his horses out through the gates.

Violet leaned back against the seat and drew a shaky breath. "You are saving my life."

He shot her a quick grin. "A coincidence. I am also endeavouring to save my own."

"Lady Redgrave's husband?" she asked, clinging to the side as the curricle swayed dangerously.

"Among others...."

"You do live, do you not, my lord?"

"No more so than you, apparently. From whom do you flee, my girl?"

Violet made a hopeless gesture. "All of them. I am found out, you see. And I cannot face Lady Hippolyta. Clarissa says she is a fire-breathing dragon when aroused, and this must arouse her for sure."

Bentley, his eyes on the dark road ahead, nodded sympathetically. "I have had experience of her sharp tongue."

"'Tis true, 'She speaks poniards, and every word stabs.'"

"Aye, and 'if her breath were as terrible as her terminations, there were no living near her; she would infect to the north star.'"

Violet choked on a spurt of nervous laughter as he completed her quote, and he beamed down at her. "That's better. What will you do when we reach Branleigh?"

"I shall gather up my essentials and leave a note informing Simpson so that she may get quickly away.

She has been helping me. I could never have attempted this masquerade without her assistance.''

A mist began to fall, though lightly, and Bentley reached under the seat for a robe to pull over their knees. Violet thanked him, and knew her words to be inadequate. Once more a knight in shining armour bearing the arms of the House of Frome had come to her rescue. If only he could have been the man with the flaming red hair. . . . Of course he hadn't, like Lochinvar, tossed her across his saddle-bow and carried her off, but owing to the inclement weather, an open-fronted curricle with a hood was far more comfortable.

"Tell me," he said suddenly. "How did you come to be involved in this imbroglio? What was your real reason for trying to steal my—Letty's—brooch? It could not be for love of that pipsqueak!''

"Oh, no. But we were not going to steal it. Monty swore to me that he only wished to borrow it, and then Clarissa said that was perfect, because she had been invited to Branleigh to announce her betrothal to Montrose. Only he wished to marry me—and do you know, now that I have had time to think, I believe she and Edward had it all planned before I ever came home from the library. And then, in the ballroom just now, a woman came up to Lady Hippolyta. You can imagine what she had to say.''

Bentley felt a trifle confused. "Never," he replied, "in a hundred years.''

"Why, she told all. That Clarissa and Edward were seen on the road to Gretna Green, so of course I had to leave. I was so frightened I simply ran out of the room and down the stairs and escaped into the courtyard.''

''Without losing a slipper, I trust?''

''A slipper? Oh, yes.'' She giggled, almost herself again. ''Indeed, I must have resembled that poor maiden, except that I was not dancing with my Prince Charming at the fatal moment.''

''My apologies. I was so hard put dodging the wicked stepsister that I could not get to you.''

She giggled again. It was amazing, the effect this man had on her, making her feel so secure and safe while her world crashed about her.

''Is that why you left the ball?'' she asked. ''I declare, I do not blame you in the least. Not after seeing that gown.''

Bentley shuddered. ''Indeed. I know not why a female should wish to make such a spectacle of herself. You, on the other hand, are exquisite tonight. The very pink of perfection. 'O thou art fairer than the evening air Clad in the beauty of a thousand stars.' ''

She fell suddenly silent, while Bentley concentrated on the handling of the ribbons. A bank of clouds hid the moon and it was difficult, without his glasses, to make out the road. He could not wear them even if he'd wished, for the lenses would rapidly coat with mist. How long, he wondered, had he to keep up this devilish disguise? Did he dare speak? Jouncing over a muddy and rutted road in a bounding curricle, behind a pair of mettlesome horses, was not the time to confess all to a lady who might not take kindly to his deception.

Nor was it the time to propose marriage to that same lady, even though the words were trembling in his throat. That was a task for a quiet moment, and for the use of both his arms. He would have to explain so many things. If only he had trusted her and told her long before; he could kick himself for not doing so! But the end of his charade was fast approaching—at least, the end of this ride. They had reached the gates of Branleigh.

He turned up the drive and pulled his team to a stop before the great front doors.

"You'd best go inside. You'll catch a chill in that flimsy gown if you have to walk from the stable. "I'll go on and put up the horses."

"Yes, thank you." Violet hopped out and ran up the front stairs as the curricle moved on around the house.

She plied the heavy knocker and waited. After a few minutes, she knocked again and tried the door. It was bolted. No one was inside. All the servants would be at the Annual Domestics' Ball at Warburton, and every window and door at Branleigh would be secured until Hepworth came home with his keys.

As she stood on the steps, wondering what on earth she was to do, the drenching rain came down.

CHAPTER ELEVEN

As BENTLEY DROVE his curricle around to the stable yard, it occurred to him that Branleigh House was totally dark. Surely there should be a light somewhere. He tried to peer into the windows of the kitchen as he passed. Were there no servants still up and about? The evening was young.

An ominous feeling crept over him. The evening was indeed young and all the domestics were very much up and about—in the Barracks Hall at Warburton Castle. Though someone must have been left behind at Branleigh. The house would be bolted, but surely there would be a guard.

Ah! There was a light in the carriage house. The stable hands would be there. He pulled up in the yard.

"Hoy!" he shouted. No one answered. Jumping lightly down, he investigated, and discovered the guardians of Branleigh. Three men lay in a stupor on a pile of hay in the corner, with several bottles of Ralston's best brandy empty on the floor beside them. Just as well. He had need of secrecy.

Leading his team inside, he hitched them to a post, still harnessed, for he had a hunch he might have need of them again this night. Dropping a forkful of hay before them, he headed back to the yard.

To make the evening complete, the light mist had become a downpour. Turning up his collar, he dashed to rescue Violet.

She sat huddled on the steps under the flickering light of the shielded flambeaus at the entrance. When she saw him, she jumped to her feet.

"We can't get in!" she cried. "I forgot—they are *all* gone to the ball! Oh, what shall I do?"

Bentley caught her waving hands and pressed them to his wet waistcoat. "There, there, calm down. I'll see that you get home."

"But I can't go home! Not after helping in Clarissa's escapade."

"I'll take you to Frome. You'll be safe with Letty."

"Lady Denville? You think *she* would take *me* in?"

"Why ever not? This whole mishmash is all her fault, you must know. If she hadn't gambled ... But, Violet, before we go, I must somehow get in and retrieve that confounded brooch."

He hesitated, looking down at her rain-streaked face. "I'm sorry if that ruins your plans to help Montrose, but after all, it is Letitia's brooch."

The reminder that she was Montrose's wife was the final straw. Violet broke down, tears joining the rain that streamed down her cheeks.

"I don't want to help M-Montrose!" she wailed. "And my hair is all uncurled—Clarissa's b-beautiful ball gown is completely ruined and I didn't get to dance even once!"

Bentley scooped her into his arms. "You shall dance for the rest of your life. A ball every night if you wish."

She didn't seem to hear him, pulling away to spread her bedraggled skirts. "Only look at Clarissa's lovely gown!"

"I'll buy you another, even prettier than this one."

That arrested her attention. She *was* being offered the fateful *carte blanche!* She stared at him, shocked. "My Lord Denville, it would not be the thing! I cannot!"

"Yes, you can," said Bentley, girding his courage. "I've been meaning to tell you about that, only there hasn't been an opportune moment." He swept off his hat. "Violet—"

For the first time since they arrived she really looked at him, and her eyes widened. "Denville," she interrupted, her words uncertain. "What is happening to your hair?"

"My hair?"

"It is dripping black all over your neckcloth!"

"Damn," said Bentley, jamming his hat down in an effort to contain the melting pomade. "All over my best evening tucker, and I'll lay you anything the stains will never come out. My valet will be furious."

Violet reached out a fascinated finger and rubbed a dribble of black goo from his cheek. "Your valet did this?"

"No, no. I did it. Old Beecham would never have approved. That's why I have this new chap. Or not exactly why. He was sort of forced on me."

Violet had made an earth-shaking discovery in the wavering gas-light. "Your hair is *red!* You—you are not Denville, you are Bentley Frome!"

"I say, I hope you do not mind too much." He shuffled his feet in the large puddle that was forming around them. "I haven't the title, you know. No chance of it now that old Hildebrand is setting up his nursery."

She didn't speak, but gazed at him openmouthed.

"I'm all out of the running," he went on, watching her with dawning hope. "You really wouldn't like being a countess, anyway. It's a beastly nuisance, all those social engagements—"

"You are Bentley! You are not Denville!"

He eyed her uneasily. It was hard to see her expression without his spectacles and under the uncertain light of the flambeaus in the rain.

"You are Bentley, not Denville!"

"Yes, you've said that several times. I've been trying to tell you for the past day or two, but we kept being interrupted."

"Oh!" she moaned. "I thought I'd fallen in love with a married man!" And so she had married Montrose.... It was too late!

"Violet—say that again—can you love me? Tell me you do."

She was in his arms. How could she tell him? The black dye dripped down, ruining the remains of Clarissa's fairy-tale gown while he held her close. He made comforting noises and she sobbed her heart out for what might have been. The rain poured over them and Violet welcomed it. It seemed fitting.

After a while Bentley raised his head. "This is all well and good, my love, but we are getting a trifle soaked. I suggest we repair to shelter."

He led her around Branleigh House, to the harness room, not the main carriage house, splashing through puddles that soon destroyed what was left of Clarissa's dancing slippers. Once inside, Violet bent to remove them, tears spilling down her chin.

Bentley was searching for a lantern. "Best keep your shoes on; no saying what you may step in."

She glanced down at her feet. What did it matter? Her life was ruined, and it was all her own fault. Oh, why had she gone through with that clandestine wedding? If only she had not been so convinced it was the one way to save herself from the charms of a married man!

The pungent odours of old leather, assorted grains, fresh hay and warm wet horses assailed her nostrils and she took a deep breath, wondering why she bothered to breathe. Bentley found a lantern hanging on a hook by the door. He took out his tinder-box and lit it. The burning whale oil sent up an acrid plume of grey, greasy smoke, and it seemed quite appropriate to her mood.

Taking off his hat, Bentley smoothed back his red-black hair. "I'm afraid we'll be here for a while. I dare not drive all the way to London in this weather."

She shrugged. "I don't care."

He started to answer, then tipped up her chin and kissed the end of her nose. "All will come right," he said simply. "Wait here, I'd best unharness my team and stable them. It may be hours before we can leave."

Violet sat on a rolled bale of hay, crushed by the weight of her utter hopelessness. Time passed and Bentley returned, stepping back into the pool of light from the lantern. He looked odd, then she saw the reason. "You are losing your moustache!"

"Am I?" From force of habit he pressed it back in place and twirled the end.

"Oh, do get rid of the silly thing."

He peeled it off and shoved it into his pocket. "Only because it is you who asks it. Let me tell you, this is a lucky moustache, according to Letitia."

"And do you call all this luck?"

"Luck!" He drew her up and hugged her. "Good God, what luck I have had in finding you! 'Fortune, they say, doth give too much to many.'"

"Harrington." Violet nodded disconsolately, playing their game of top the quote for perhaps the last time. "'But yet she never gave enough to any.'"

"Whatever makes you say that? My love, I am drowning in luck as well as in the rain!"

Through a momentary lull in the storm, the sound of someone yelling and pounding on the oaken kitchen door penetrated to the harness room.

Bentley set her gently aside and peered out. Then, taking his spectacles from his pocket and putting them on, he looked again.

"Demme if it isn't my friend Norton." He poked out his head and shouted cheerily, "'Knock as you please, there's nobody home.' Pope," he explained to Violet.

Norton headed for their shelter, scuttling like a furious half-drowned rat.

"I walked the whole 'ellish way across the fields!" he howled. "And I can't get in!"

"Walked, did you?" Bentley, by now feeling quite above himself, shook his head. "What a pity. Had you let me know, you could have ridden with us."

This did nothing to improve Norton's temper. He muttered something under his breath as he came inside. The lantern lit his dishevelled figure and Violet gave a startled exclamation.

"It is the vicar!"

"The what?" Bentley eyed Norton with interest. "Are you a parson as well as a thief?"

"A thief! You mean he is not a parson?"

"Course I ain't no parson." Norton leered at Violet. "But 'oo am I to interfere with a gentleman's bit o' pleasure?"

About to faint, Violet sank down on the hay bale. Then she wasn't married! Montrose had deceived her!

"'Ere now, I 'ope I ain't caused no 'ardship."

"No, oh no, you have made me unbelievably happy!" She rose and threw herself into Bentley's arms. "Can you ever forgive me for being such a goosecap?" she begged. "I love you so much!"

Something was going on that Bentley didn't understand, but Violet loved him and nothing else mattered. He held her hesitantly, as though still unsure of this miracle. His chin rested on her wet headdress; the soggy ostrich-plume slopped against his cheek. He didn't care.

"I ask no more of life than this," he murmured in her ear. " 'Let the world slide, let the world go.' "

" 'A fig for care, a fig for woe,' " she completed the quote in a shaky voice and he laughed, on a triumphant note.

This did not go over well with Norton. "That'll be enough o' that smart talk," he snapped.

Bentley by now was unable to contain his exuberance. " 'Hail, fellow, well met,' " he quoted. " 'All dirty and wet: Find out if you can, Who's master, who's man.' "

"Jonathan Swift?" asked Violet, interested.

"Right." Bentley kissed her ear.

Norton glared at them sourly. "Making free in barns. I don't 'old with such like. And my name's not Swift, and I ain't nobody's man."

Bentley turned courteously to Violet. "Allow me to present Mr. Norton, my valet."

"I ain't no valet neither!" Norton snapped.

Bentley agreed. "I can certainly attest to that. I daresay you've come back for a try at the black jewellery case."

For some reason, this affected Norton strongly. Beyond speech, he merely snarled, and Bentley shook his head, sympathizing.

"I hate to add to your misfortune, but I fear you no longer have any standing in Branleigh House. Your master has been unmasked. You'll have to find some other means to seek that box."

Norton found his voice. "You're welcome to it—and its contents, too!" He yanked the black case from his pocket and threw it at Bentley's feet.

Bentley scooped up the precious case with an exultant cry.

Norton sneered and turned towards the door. "Tell Mathilda she'll find me at the tavern in the village," he ordered.

Pretending to pull at a black-streaked red forelock, Bentley bowed. "Certainly, sir. Will there be anything else, sir?"

What Norton said he could do next fortunately was incomprehensible to Violet. Bentley, however, had a working knowledge of cant. Seizing the man by the scruff of his neck and the seat of his inexpressibles, he threw him out into the rain.

"You are quite good at that," Violet approved.

Bentley scrubbed his hands on his ruined breeches, as though to remove all trace of Norton, and grinned at her.

"If a thing is once successful, it is worth repeating. And speaking of 'divers and eminent successes,' come here.... Violet, our minds are as one, and now—our hearts?"

Suddenly confused and shy, Violet tried to continue the game. "'Two friends, two bodies with one soul inspir'd!'"

"Friendship is not quite what I have in mind." With one hand, he raised her face to his and emphasized each word with a gentle touch of his lips on forehead, nose, eyes and chin. "Mr. Jonathan Swift had an excellent suggestion. 'Under this window in stormy weather... I marry this man and woman together....' Violet, will you marry me?"

Her heart seemed to swell within her, filling her with a radiant joy. She touched his cheek and completed the quote. "'Let none but Him who rules the thunder,'" she whispered softly, "'Put this man and woman asunder.'"

"Lord, there never was a woman like you." Bentley breathed the words into the straight wet hair by her ear. "Who needs to wrest a star from the sky? 'I have caught my heav'nly jewel.'"

A long and rather pleasant interlude transpired.

After a while, Violet pushed him slightly away. "Should we not open the box? That man may have removed your brooch!"

"Good lord, I hadn't thought of that." Bentley released her. With fingers that shook in spite of himself, he tripped the catch and lifted the lid of the black velvet box.

Together, they stared at the deck of cards.

"He did!" Violet exclaimed. "He has stolen the brooch and given us this instead!"

"No." Bentley tipped out the pack of pasteboards and slowly replaced it. "No. This fits too well. It is not a jewellery case, it was made to hold a deck of cards." He snapped the lid shut. "Oh, hell and the devil confound it!" he muttered. "I mean—my apologies, my love. I should not have said that."

"Don't apologize! I might have said it myself had I known the proper words."

With a rueful laugh, he dropped the box on the floor and once more drew her into his arms. "We are not yet beaten. It only means that I must somehow get into Branleigh, now while everyone is gone, and really search Ralston's rooms."

"We cannot get in until the servants return."

"There must be a window left unbolted somewhere. I'm going out to check the upper storeys."

Violet squeaked. "No, Bentley, you cannot!"

"Of course I can. The walls are most conveniently covered with ivy, made for climbing."

"No! The rain will make them slippery. You will fall! Bentley, you cannot go out and get killed just when I have found you!"

He discovered it was necessary to kiss her again. "Very well, my love. We'll wait until someone comes with a key. Then we can sneak inside to collect our belongings, and perhaps have a last chance to hunt through his bedchamber."

"Bentley," Violet began in a very small voice, "the brooch may not be in the house."

"What do you mean?"

"He showed it to me once. He took it from a little pocket in his waistcoat, where he kept his watch."

He stared down at her, thunderstruck. "Do you mean he may carry it always on his person?"

"Honestly, when I saw him hide that box in the library, I believed it held the diamond. He was so secretive!"

"You were watching? Could he have known you were there and tricked you on purpose?"

She shook her head. "He could not have known. It was that night... that night when you hid me behind the draperies. He came in after all was quiet, before you came back, and I saw him take the box from behind some books and put it in his pocket. I was sure it was the gem."

"I saw him hide it there, too." Thoughtfully, Bentley picked up the case and turned it over in his hand. "Could he have been hoaxing us all?"

"If he truly keeps the brooch on his person, there is no way for us to get it from him."

"For me to get it," Bentley corrected. "The man is dangerous, my love. Keep away from him. I do not like the look I have seen in his eyes."

Violet shivered, and he immediately took off his wet tailcoat and put it about her shoulders, taking advantage of the action to give her a hug.

"There's nothing we can do now at any rate, my love. We'll have to wait out this storm and see what comes next."

He pulled two sacks of milled grain from one of the bins for seats and set the lantern beside them.

"Piquet?" he asked, opening the case and taking out the cards. "What say you to a kiss a point? We may as well amuse ourselves until the party from the County Ball returns."

They settled down to while away the time, and to facilitate her play, Violet took her spectacles from

Clarissa's fancy reticule without thinking and put them on.

To her amazement, Bentley, who already wore his own, seemed to notice no difference in her appearance, accepting the wearing of spectacles as perfectly natural. A warm glow spread through her as the last barrier between them went down.

Bentley, still feeling quite cock-a-whoop, and more Hildebrandish by the moment, put the lucky moustache back on. He twirled it rakishly and dealt out the cards like a true gamester.

His expression changed as he handled the pasteboards. An odd note entered his voice.

"My love," he said, struggling to remain calm. "I do believe we have won after all."

CHAPTER TWELVE

"BY ALL THAT'S HOLY!" Awestruck, Bentley repeated his words. "My love, we have won."

"Well, I have not." Violet frowned at her hand. "You cannot imagine what poor cards I hold."

"You do not care for those I dealt you?" A tremor, blended of excitement and triumph, coloured his voice. Without looking, he extracted a court-card from the deck he still held and laid it in front of her. "Then accept a king, my lady."

"You would have me cheat? Not at all the thing, my—Mr. Frome!"

He produced another card with a flourish. "You would perhaps prefer a queen?"

Violet gasped. "Bentley! How did you do that?"

"The lucky moustache has come through!" He chortled, a happy sound. "Though it is about done for. The d-dratted thing will not stick properly any more."

Violet laid down her cards and placed a soothing hand on his brow. "I fear you have at last parted with your wits."

"No, no. All is well. It is no wonder Ralston has had the devil's own luck at piquet. And it is no wonder he was at such pains to keep this black case safely hidden. Violet, these cards are fuzzed. If Ralston's cheating is revealed, he is a ruined man. We hold here the winning hand."

She gazed at him, her eyes round. "You mean—"

"Yes, my love, I do mean. I am now in a position to demand the return of Lady Denville's brooch. And we need fear no repercussions for our masquerades." He paused, looking a trifle less secure. "At least, not from Ralston. What Lady Hippolyta will have to say will be another matter."

"She will say nothing." Violet looked up from the court-cards she was studying, feeling along the edges for the tell-tale nicks. "Lady Hippolyta could not wish to have such a story broadcast to the ton. The good names of Ralston and Branleigh mean too much to her."

Bentley nodded. "I trust you are right. Now if only we could get inside and don dry clothing, all would indeed be well that ends well."

As if in answer to his wish, the crunching of gravel beneath wheels and hooves could be heard above the pelting rain. Bentley opened the door and peered outside into the dark stable yard.

"I doubt these are relief troops," he said. "It appears to be a curricle returning, not a carriage bearing butlers and house keys. We have yet some time to wait."

He returned to Violet, caught her up in his arms, and spent several minutes profitably, murmuring phrases he would ordinarily consider asinine into her receptive ears. Their spectacles bumped when they kissed, but they overcame that minor problem by taking them off.

The door to the harness room was flung open and Lord Ralston entered, shaking rainwater from his many-caped driving coat. He stopped dead and stared at them.

Bentley released Violet with some reluctance, and greeted him cheerfully. "I see you could not get in either."

"So!" Ralston spoke through clenched teeth. "Sir John spoke the truth! You are Bentley Frome and not Denville at all."

"How do you do?" Bentley bowed courteously. "Yes, my name is Frome. However, my errand here is the same as my brother's would have been. I am come to redeem Lady Denville's brooch."

For a minute, Ralston did not speak. His bulging eyes had taken in the open black case and the cards scattered on the floor. His face slowly purpled and a vein in his temple began throbbing dangerously, threatening apoplexy.

"Give me those cards!" His lordship barely breathed the words.

Bentley stooped and gathered up the king and queen he had dealt to Violet. "Not until you return my sister's brooch," he said quietly.

Ralston snapped his fingers impatiently and held out his hand. "My cards."

Bentley stood his ground, conscious suddenly of Violet slipping behind him. He held out his own hand. "The brooch, please. I have examined your cards."

"That is unfortunate." Ralston reached into one of his deep coat pockets and revealed a long-barrelled duelling pistol. "But how fortunate that I carry my Mantons in my curricle and had the forethought to arm myself with them when I saw a suspicious light in my carriage house." He aimed the gun at Bentley's chest. "I must insist on your giving those cards to me at once."

"No," said Bentley. "Not until you return the brooch. And maybe not then," he added thoughtfully. "You really should not be allowed to continue bilking innocent pigeons."

With a deadly clicking sound, Ralston cocked the pistol, and for a second, Bentley hesitated and licked his lips. Violet tried to step in front of him and he thrust her firmly back. "Stay behind me."

She clung to his arm instead and Ralston smiled.

"You are correct to fear me, Lady Clarissa. I am quite prepared to fire if necessary."

"I am not Clarissa!" Violet announced, defiant in her position of comparative safety beside Bentley. "I am not going to marry Montrose and no one can make me!"

Ralston's eyebrows rose. "So I have harboured not one but two impostors." He shrugged. "It makes no difference now, since you both know my secret. I shall have that deck of cards, Frome. One way or another. I am afraid my livelihood depends on my winnings.

And you, my girl, Clarissa or not, will have to go as well.''

"Go where?'' Bentley demanded, stalling for time. "We are not leaving without that brooch.'' But what could he do? Ralston stood with his back to the door and there was no other way out. Could they ease around him? Or better yet, disarm the man? Bentley shot a glance around the room but saw no weapon within reach. The far too tidy stablehands had hung their tools neatly upon the back wall. There were several grain barrels, but by the time he managed to tip one over and roll it across the room, Ralston would probably have shot him. He'd be thus unable to rescue Violet.

Ralston seemed to have read his thoughts. He smiled again, but there was no humour in the cold thinning of his lips.

"My cards, if you please.''

"Pick them up yourself.''

"And take my eyes from you? Oh, no. At least not yet. I can retrieve them afterwards, of course, but I rather thought you'd like to live a few minutes longer.''

Violet gave a tiny squeak and Bentley pulled her against him.

Ralston looked at them, his features expressing a mild interest. "Blows the wind in that quarter? I see I need not have destroyed that vase. You were not pursuing my son's wealthy fiancée, but your own little Cyprian.''

Bentley clenched his fists. "I ought to plant you a facer!"

The pistol waved negligently. "I think you will not."

"And I suppose it was you who dropped that potted palm on me as well."

"You must hold me blameless there. If anyone tried to brain you with a palm tree, it was probably Redgrave, thinking you were planning an affair with Beatrix. Beastly temper that man has." He moved the gun slightly, looking a bit uneasy himself. "Enough. But perhaps you'd care to take time for a tender farewell."

"You would not dare murder us." Bentley gave Violet a reassuring squeeze.

Ralston moved the gun slightly. "Oh, I am not above shooting you both, you know. I have come home to find prowlers in my carriage house. I shall be devastated later to learn it was a pair of my guests in a clandestine meeting. Though not as devastated as you'll be, of course."

Quite occupied with his melodrama in the harness room, Ralston apparently did not hear the arrival of another carriage. Bentley tensed, holding Violet tighter. If he could keep the man distracted...

"You would not dare," he repeated, raising his voice and praying to be heard outside. "My body will be easily identified. How do you mean to explain the combination of my presence and your possession of the Denville diamond?"

Ralston frankly laughed. "My dear boy! You have supplied that answer yourself and a witness to your tale. I already told you I have made quite sure that anyone of any importance knows I won the Denville diamond fair and square. And as for you, Sir John has already put it about that your hoax was a disguise, a chance to romp with your ladybird in the country.''

"Ah, but I am not Denville. I have not his reputation for larks, so no one would believe it of me.''

"I venture to say it shall be an easy matter to convince them. There is nothing that satisfies the Polite World more than a good scandal." Ralston shook his head, almost sadly. "A pity. And a lesson for all. One should not venture out of one's class. It so frequently leads to grievous accidents such as this will be. How lucky I brought in both loaded pistols." He moved the gun in his hand slightly. "I believe good manners decree that the lady goes first.''

He aimed the gun at Violet and Bentley shoved her behind him as the harness-room door creaked open. Ralston spun about, pointing the gun at the newcomer.

Lady Hippolyta stood in the doorway, a dripping mountain of lilac satin.

"Put that silly pistol away, you nodcock!'' she thundered, and such was the power of Ralston's years of conditioning at her hands that he almost dropped the gun.

Bentley thrust Violet roughly out of the way and tackled the man about the knees, throwing him to the paved floor. He grappled frantically for the hand that still clutched the pistol. It waved about in the air.

"Be careful with that thing!" Lady Hippolyta ordered. "Do you want to kill us all?"

Her only answer came in grunts from the wrestling men and she attempted to flatten herself against the door, but her figure was not built for flattening. Receiving a sharp clout on the shin from one of the flailing legs, she sought other refuge, and with amazing agility for one of her build, she clambered up on one of the low chests filled with odd pieces of harness.

Violet hopped about the struggling figures, the black case clutched in her hand as a weapon, looking for an opportunity to land a blow on Ralston.

"Here, that's no use!" Lady Hippolyta handed her an old wooden bucket, partially filled with broken brasses and rusty bits of metal. "Crown him with this."

Violet accepted it without question and raised it high, waiting for the right moment. But the bottom fell out of the ancient pail, raining metal scraps indiscriminately over both men. A heavy buckle caught Bentley in the eye and he lost his grip on Ralston's wrist.

The loosed pistol swung towards Lady Hippolyta, who yanked a handy manure shovel from the wall behind her. She brought the flat side down on her nephew's head with all her weight behind it. Before he could collect the scattered wits in his ringing skull, Violet wrenched the gun from his hand and threw it across the room. Bentley, on top for a change, sat on Ralston's chest and pinned both his arms to the floor.

"Pockets!" he yelled at Violet. "A pair of Mantons, he said. He will have another pistol."

She found the gun and held it against his lordship's left ear with a shaking hand. "Do I just pull the trigger?" she asked. "I have never fired one of these."

Ralston suddenly lay very still. "For God's sake, take that from her," he whispered through frozen lips. "It has a hair trigger."

Bentley straddled Ralston's recumbent body until Violet put the pistol in his hand. Then he rose carefully, keeping aim on the man who, with equal caution, got to his feet.

Lady Hippolyta, grunting with satisfaction, took in the scene, her eyes travelling from Violet's ruined finery to Bentley's somewhat picturesque figure. The false moustache hung by a thread, and his half-red, half-black hair straggled over his dye-streaked forehead. She stumped down onto the floor, her bright bird's eyes alive with interest.

"Well, well," she said. "What have we here?"

Bentley sketched a bow, still holding the pistol on Ralston. "Bentley Frome, my lady, at your service. Pray accept my apologies, but believe me, the disguise was necessary."

She nodded and gave a complacent chuckle. "So you are not Denville after all. No wonder my maid servants have not, all in a group, given notice. To tell truth, I had begun to wonder at your restraint." She turned to Violet, looking slightly disappointed. "Then I suppose you are not one of his bits o' fancy, either."

"No," said Violet firmly.

"Who are you, then? I thought you one of Denville's doxies when I discovered you were not Clarissa, but if this is *Bentley* Frome... And you speak like a lady, my dear."

Violet curtsied; it seemed the thing to do. "I am Clarissa's cousin, Violet Langford, and I am deeply sorry to have deceived you in this manner, my lady. But I promised Clarissa to help her elope with Sir Edward Moore. She feared instant pursuit unless she was known to be at Branleigh, so I had to take her place."

Lady Hippolyta humphed. "She did not wish to marry Montrose, I suspect. Indeed, I suppose I cannot blame her."

"Enough of this!" Ralston had straightened his disarranged clothing, and now tried to recapture his dignity. He was becoming restive, and Bentley still held his pistol. "I'll tell you who they are. They are brigands come to rob us! Cutthroats! Jewel thieves!" He bit his tongue, sensing he had brought up a subject best ignored.

Lady Hippolyta eyed him calmly. "I collect this is all about that diamond you won. The Denville heirloom, is it not?" She raised questioning brows at Bentley.

Wisely, he refrained from mentioning that the stone in question was paste. He merely stated that he had come with the intention of redeeming Letitia's brooch, as had been agreed by both parties. Now, he told her, Ralston had gone back on his word and refused to give it up.

"You blithering idiot," she remarked dispassionately to her nephew. "Is a fortune worth being had up for murder?"

"They left me no alternative," he blustered.

But she had noticed the pack of cards, now scattered over the floor by the commotion. "I seem to have interrupted a game. Were you playing again for the gem?" She bent with some difficulty and tried to pick up one of the court-cards.

Ralston paled. "They are mine!" Ignoring the pistol, he dropped to his knees and began scrabbling about, gathering them up. He stopped, finding the muzzle of his Manton inches from his nose.

"That's right." Bentley nodded. "But I fear," he went on, "you will have to give up that form of gaming." He held out his hand. "Give them to me."

"No," said Ralston.

Bentley blinked. "But I have the pistol."

"You won't fire it."

"What's all this about these cards?" Lady Hippolyta demanded.

Bentley started to speak and Ralston yelped.

"No!"

"I'll tell her," offered Violet. "I believe your aunt has a right to know about your late activities."

Ralston sagged where he knelt and Lady Hippolyta turned her penetrating gaze on Bentley. "You tell me. I collect you are the one most concerned."

Bentley shrugged. "It is a simple matter. Lord Ralston has been playing piquet with a marked deck, and by so cheating, he won Letty's—Lady Denville's—brooch. She wants it back."

"I see." Lady Hippolyta considered her nephew meditatively, her lip curling in distaste. She turned her attention back to Bentley and Violet. "This requires careful handling if we are not all to go down in infamy. I trust you two are the only witnesses to his perfidy?"

"As far as we know."

"Then, I hope, if my nephew returns the diamond, there will be no need to create a scandal, one that would reveal Lady Denville's gaming, not to mention heap disgrace on Branleigh?" Lady Hippolyta held out an imperious hand to Ralston. "Lady Denville's brooch, if you please."

Ralston hesitated. "I want my cards."

"Not a chance," said Bentley. "You may consider them the price of our silence."

The dowager's hand was still outstretched. Ralston slowly reached into his waistcoat pocket and removed the brooch. It glittered in the lantern light as brilliantly as if the stone had been genuine, and Violet, seeing it once again, caught her breath at its beauty. Lady Hippolyta pried the brooch from Ralston's reluctant fingers and passed it to Bentley, who tucked it away in his own pocket with a long sigh of relief.

Attempting a careless manner, Ralston headed for the door. "I should have known better than to get mixed up with you wretched Denvilles. I wish you may both go to the devil!"

Bentley, sober-faced, made him an elegant bow. "You may be sure I will pass your message along. And now good-night. 'A thousand times good-night!' " Ever polite, he held the door open and Ralston strode out into the rain.

"Good," said the dowager. "I see it is still in a downpour. A nice wetting should restore his reason. You need fear him no longer."

Violet knelt and collected the fallen cards, replacing them in the black case. She sat back on her heels, looking at them uncertainly. "What should we do with these?"

Lady Hippolyta, straining a bit, bent to take the black box from her. "I think these had best be kept in my possession. You may be sure I have a use for them. I have a strong desire to see that Ralston toes the line in the future."

Bentley coughed gently. "I do not wish to argue, but have you a safe deposit?"

A smug smile creased her fat cheeks. "The safest. I will send the box at once to my man of business in London, with a letter describing the contents to be opened should anything happen to any one of us. My nephew shall be informed of that fact as soon as it is delivered into my solicitor's keeping."

Bentley helped Violet to her feet, holding both her hands in his, and Lady Hippolyta gazed at them benevolently.

"My children," she said. "This was all a foolish waste of time. You should have come straight to me in the first place."

"We were afraid to," Violet explained. "Clarissa told me you were a dragon!" She flushed at her tactless *faux pas,* clapping a hand to her mouth.

Lady Hippolyta stared at her, amazed. "Me? Why, I am the gentlest, most understanding female on earth. Only see how kindly I have dealt with my erring nephew!" She turned and lumbered towards the door, yawning delicately behind one pudgy hand. "I am going to my bed. All this excitement is wearing to one of my age."

"Ah, you have a key to the house, then?" Bentley asked, on a note of hope.

"Of course not," she said. "Hepworth keeps all the keys."

Violet giggled. "Oh, dear, then I fear you are in for a wait."

Lady Hippolyta looked at her.

"The Annual Domestics' Ball," Violet explained. "The house is bolted until your butler returns."

The dowager stood for a moment, silent. Then she shrugged philosophically. With a gusty wheeze, she settled her bulk onto the chest containing old harness leathers and tossed the black box to Bentley.

"In that case—" she heaved another sigh "—deal me a hand, my boy."

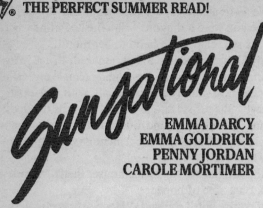

Take 4 bestselling love stories FREE

Plus get a FREE surprise gift!

Special Limited-time Offer

Mail to
Harlequin Reader Service®
3010 Walden Avenue
P.O. Box 1867
Buffalo, N.Y. 14269-1867

YES! Please send me 4 free Harlequin Regency Romance™ novels and my free surprise gift. Then send me 4 brand-new novels every other month. Bill me at the low price of $2.64 each—a savings of 31¢ apiece off cover prices. There are no shipping, handling or other hidden costs. I understand that accepting the books and gift places me under no obligation ever to buy any books. I can always return a shipment and cancel at any time. Even if I never buy another book from Harlequin, the 4 free books and the surprise gift are mine to keep forever.

248 BPA AC9G

Name	(PLEASE PRINT)	
Address		Apt. No.
City	State	Zip

This offer is limited to one order per household and not valid to present Harlequin Regency Romance™ subscribers. Terms and prices are subject to change. Sales tax applicable in N.Y.

REG-BPA2DR   © 1990 Harlequin Enterprises Limited

Back by Popular Demand

Janet Dailey
Americana

A romantic tour of America through fifty favorite Harlequin Presents, each set in a different state researched by Janet and her husband, Bill. A journey of a lifetime in one cherished collection.

In August, don't miss the exciting states featured in:

Title #13 — ILLINOIS
       The Lyon's Share

   #14 — INDIANA
       The Indy Man

Available wherever
Harlequin books are sold.

JD-AUG